COWBOY UNDER FIRE

BY
CARLA CASSIDY

First Published in Great Britain 2016
By Mills & Boon, an imprint of HarperCollins*Publishers*
1 London Bridge Street, London, SE1 9GF

© 2016 Carla Bracale

ISBN: 978-0-263-91928-8

18-0116

Our policy is to use papers that are natural, renewable and recyclable products and made from wood grown in sustainable forests.The logging and manufacturing processes conform to the legal environmental regulations of the country of origin.

Printed and bound in Spain
by CPI, Barcelona

"You think I'm in danger." It was a statement, not a question.

Forest hesitated a moment and then nodded somberly. "Even though you don't remember it, you were viciously attacked. Until we know why or by whom, I don't want you alone anywhere."

"Does that mean I've just gained a bodyguard?" Patience asked.

He smiled. "Yeah, and I already know you don't like it, but until somebody is in jail for attacking you or you finish up your work and leave here, you have your own personal bodyguard."

"But you have your own work to do here at the ranch," she protested.

"During the days when you're in the tent doing your thing, I'll be in the corral working with the horse. When you're safe in your room, I'll be in mine. If you decide to go anywhere for any reason, you need to make sure I'm with you."

His gaze was once again somber. "This isn't optional, Patience."

* * *

Be sure to check out the next books in this exciting series:

Cowboys of Holiday Ranch—Where sun, earth and hard work turn men into rugged cowboys. . .and irresistible heroes!

Carla Cassidy is a *New York Times* bestselling author who has written more than one hundred books for Mills & Boon. Carla believes the only thing better than curling up with a good book to read is sitting down at the computer with a good story to write. She's looking forward to writing many more books and bringing hours of pleasure to readers.

Chapter 1

She cast a tiny shadow, but was as snappy as a ticked-off Chihuahua. Forest Stevens cast a huge shadow but rarely got riled up about anything. Still, since the moment the petite Dr. Patience Forbes had arrived on the Holiday Ranch, she'd fired him up in a way he hadn't felt before.

Not that he'd done anything about it...at least not yet. Despite the fact that she'd been on the property for the past three weeks, he had yet to do much of anything except tip his black hat as she stalked back and forth from her room next to his to the blue tent where she worked.

He was aware of the importance of her work. As a forensic anthropologist she'd been brought to the ranch by the discovery of a mass grave beneath an old shed that had been damaged in the spring by a tornado. The pit of bones had been unearthed when the ranch hands were tearing down the shed after the storm.

He now stood just outside the tent where she and her assistant, a middle-aged man named Dr. Devon Lewison, had been dealing with the bones of the dead in an attempt to put skeletons back together again and gather information so that identities could potentially be established or a clue to the killer might be discovered.

For the entire length of time that she'd been on the ranch, she hadn't interacted with anyone except Devon and Chief of Police Dillon Bowie. She worked from dawn until dusk and didn't take her meals in the cowboy dining room.

Forest hoped to change some of that. For a man who was six-four and strong as an ox, a ridiculous nervousness raced through him as he drew a deep breath and stepped in front of the doorway of the tent.

She immediately whipped around, her red, shoulderlength curls dancing with her movement as her green eyes narrowed in obvious irritation. "You're blocking my light, cowboy."

Moving left or right wouldn't change the fact that he completely filled up the tent entrance. "My name isn't cowboy, it's Forest… Forest Stevens." He quickly swept his hat off his head, as if that polite gesture would somehow turn her deep frown into a pleasant smile. It didn't.

"Okay, Forest Stevens, what's the problem?"

She stood before a stainless-steel table where dried brown bones were laid out in the quasi-pattern of a human being. Forest averted his gaze from the remnants of death to her.

"No problem," he replied easily. "You're staying in the room next to mine. I just figured it was about time we spoke."

"Good. Now we've spoken. Goodbye." She dismissed him by turning her slender back on him.

Forest stepped out the tent entrance and heaved a sigh of frustration. He shouldn't be dismayed by her curtness. At least he knew not to take it personally. She hadn't been friendly with anyone on the ranch. Even Dillon called her Dr. Dreadful or the dragon lady behind her back.

Dusty Crawford, the youngest cowboy working on the ranch, stood just a few feet away, and his dimples flashed as he grinned at Forest. "Ah, cut off right at the knees," he said. "At least that brings you down to my height."

"Very funny," Forest replied and set his hat back on his head. "Besides, I wasn't cut off anywhere. All I wanted to do was introduce myself to her and I accomplished that."

The two men headed for the stables. "Dillon says the woman breathes fire whenever she opens her mouth."

And a fine mouth it was, Forest thought. Perfectly formed with just enough plump to look utterly kissable. He grimaced and shoved the thought aside.

"He also says she must eat nails for breakfast and spits them out with a sharp sting with her temper. Even Cassie insists the woman has ice in her veins," Dusty continued.

Cassie. There was still a dull ache in Forest's heart when he thought of his new young boss. Three months ago Cass Holiday had been killed in a tornado that had ripped through the property. She'd left behind twelve cowboys who had loved her like a mother and a legacy of high standards and loyalty.

Cass had left the successful ranch to her niece, Cassie Peterson, a New York artist and shop owner. Over the last two months Cassie had surprised them all. With the help of foreman Adam Benson, she had jumped right in to learn the ropes of running such a big operation.

She wasn't the woman her aunt had been, but she appeared to be trying her best to learn all there was to know about ranch life. Still, the cowboys working the Holiday spread considered themselves Cass's cowboys, not Cassie's men.

"Are you going into town tonight?" Dusty asked, pulling Forest from his thoughts. "It's Saturday night, so I figure I'll grab dinner at the café and then maybe amble over to the Watering Hole for a few beers."

"I think I'll just stick around here," Forest replied. "You know you could always eat in the cowboy dining room right here and then head out to the Watering Hole," he said in mock innocence.

"I'm just kinda in the mood for Daisy's Saturday night meat loaf special, and I know Cookie is planning on burgers tonight."

"Tell the truth, you couldn't care less about meat loaf— you just want to go to the café to try again to sweeten up Trisha," Forest said, referring to one of the waitresses who worked on Saturday nights.

Dusty heaved a disheartened sigh. "I've been trying

to sweeten up that woman for months, and she's having nothing to do with it."

"Then why don't you just give it up? There are plenty of other single women in Bitterroot just waiting for a young buck like you to take an interest in them."

They reached the stables and both headed to the saw-horses where saddles were slung across the tops. "She gives me mixed messages," Dusty said. "She isn't married and yet she doesn't date anyone. I sometimes see her watching me when she thinks I'm not looking. I'm not a bad-looking guy, right?"

"You've got a certain charm about you with all that blond hair and those deep dimples, but you're definitely not my type," Forest replied with a wry grin.

Dusty grabbed his saddle by the horn and pulled it off the sawhorse. "One of these days she's either going to tell me to get lost or agree to go out with me. Until one of those things happens, I'll be eating meat loaf at the café on Saturday nights."

Forest watched as Dusty headed for the stall where his horse was housed. He feared that Dusty was caught up more in the challenge of the chase than guided by any real feelings for the pretty waitress.

Time would tell how things worked out for Dusty and Trisha. *Not my problem*, Forest thought and grabbed his own saddle and headed for his horse, Thunder. Thunder was a large brown horse, but it took a big horse to carry a big cowboy.

Dusty rode up to Forest. "What about the barn dance next Friday night? Are you planning on going?"

"Haven't made up my mind yet," Forest replied.

"Abe always throws a heck of a party."

"I know," Forest agreed. Over the years Forest had been to many of Abe Breckinridge's barn parties. It was always a good time for all who attended.

"You know most of us will go. We need somebody who can carry Sawyer to the back of a truck at the end of the night."

Forest grinned as he thought of fellow ranch hand Sawyer Quincy. The man rarely drank, but when he did, it didn't take much alcohol to put him totally under the table.

"I'm sure if I don't go then somebody else will manage to get Sawyer home safe and sound."

Dusty nodded and left the stables. It took Forest only minutes to saddle up and ride out into the bright morning and head toward the distant pasture. Today he had to check out the cattle stock and make sure they all appeared healthy and no prey had attacked them overnight.

There were eleven cowboys currently working the ranch. They had lost one a month ago when Lucas Taylor had moved on to a small ranch of his own with his girlfriend Nicolette and her son, Sammy. The two were getting married in a couple of weeks.

Then, another ranch cowboy, Nick Coleman, had also found love and moved off the ranch to a nice two-story house in the small nearby town of Bitterroot, but Nick continued to work here from dawn until dusk and then went home to his wife, Adrienne, each evening.

Lucky Lucas and lucky Nick, they had both found

love and were building a future with the special women who had captured their hearts.

It didn't take long for Forest to reach the large herd of Angus cattle. He waved to Flint McCay who rode along the fence line, checking for breaks.

The mid-July sun was hot on his back as he cut through the cattle, looking for any that might appear sick or wounded. This was the core wealth of the ranch—the livestock and the contacts Cass had made in the beef industry. They had built Cass a small empire and a respected name in the state and beyond.

Thoughts of the woman who had taken him on as a homeless teenager vanished as thoughts of another woman filled his head. He had no idea why he was so intrigued with Dr. Patience Forbes.

She'd been a prickly pear since the moment she'd arrived, not even pretending to be friendly with anyone on the ranch. When she finished her work for the day, she disappeared into her small bunk room, not to be seen again until morning when she was back at work. The only person she obviously had a relationship with was her assistant.

In all the years of working and living on the Holiday Ranch and interacting with the people of Bitterroot, Oklahoma, Forest had never had any real feelings for a woman.

He'd dated a bit over the years, had slept with a couple of willing partners, but his heart had never been involved with anyone. Of course, he wasn't looking for a heart match with Patience. He was just curious about her, that was all.

Curiosity killed the cat, a little voice whispered in the back of his head. He smiled inwardly. He didn't believe Patience would be his death, but he definitely wasn't ready to admit defeat already where she was concerned.

The tall, big-shouldered cowboy with the rich dark hair and piercing blue eyes had definitely broken Patience's concentration. And concentration was vital for the work she was doing.

"Let's take a break," she said to Devon. "We'll get back to work in about half an hour."

"Then I'm heading into the trailer where it's cool," Devon replied.

Patience raised a hand to wave him out of the tent and then sat on a nearby chair. At the foot of the chair was a small cooler. She opened it and shoved aside a bag of cheese puffs to retrieve a cold soda.

She rubbed the cool can across her forehead where the beginning of a headache attempted to blossom. This was the most challenging job she'd been handed since becoming a part of the Oklahoma City Police Department and in addition to teaching classes at the university.

She'd worked plenty of cases where bones had been found and the police needed her expertise in aging them and looking for anything that might provide identification.

But this particular burial site had six bodies that had dissolved to nothing but bones. As the bodies had deteriorated, the bones had all collapsed together, forcing her to work six different puzzles. It had been easy to know that there were six bodies by the six skulls.

At least the young woman's body that had been found here along with the others had been identified and her recent murder solved, leaving Patience only the grave-yard of old bones to deal with.

She popped open the top of her soda and took a long drink. The tent interior was hot and would only get hotter as the July days got longer and the dog days of August moved in. But she couldn't allow a fan to blow or any equipment to change the atmosphere, to subtly move the dirt or taint the crime scene and the six skel-etons in the same grave that could only be the result of murder.

Once again she thought of the cowboy who had broken her concentration. Forest. Forest Stevens. She couldn't help but have noticed him around the ranch since she'd arrived.

He rode taller in the saddle than the other men and his incredible shoulders tapered into a slim waist, and she suspected his legs were firmly muscled beneath his worn well-fitting jeans.

She frowned. Why had he stopped to talk to her at all? She'd made it clear by action and more than a hint of snarky attitude that she had no interest in making new friends or acquaintances while she was here.

She had a job to do, and when this job was over she'd move on to the next one. Besides, she didn't do friends, she didn't do lovers. She did bones.

Bones spoke to her in words that didn't hurt. They

gave her facts, not lies. She liked her bones far more than she liked people.

Still, she had to give Forest Stevens props for facing down the dragon lady. She shook her head ruefully and then took another sip of the refreshing soda. She knew how everyone on the ranch talked about her behind her back. She didn't care. She wasn't here for warm and fuzzy feelings, she was here to help the local chief of police solve a crime.

By the time she'd finished her soda, Devon had returned from the long trailer that held not only scientific equipment and a mini-lab in the front, but also a tiny kitchenette, bathroom and bunk in the back. The vehicle was hooked up to both a generator and a water line running from the house.

Most of the time when they traveled to burial scenes, Devon stayed in the recreational-vehicle-turned-lab, and Patience ended up staying in a nearby motel or rented room and driving back and forth to the scene.

She'd been told before she arrived here that there was a room on the premises where she could stay. She had a room in what the cowboys called the cowboy motel, a sprawling twelve-unit building that housed all of the ranch hands who worked on the ranch.

On the back side of the building was a large dining area where a man named Cookie prepared meals. She didn't eat there—not because she would be the only woman in the place, that wouldn't bother her, but because she didn't want to pretend that she was here for anything else but work. She didn't make small talk and she didn't attempt to play nice with the locals. There was no point.

The tedious job of removing each tiny bone and then staring at her computer screen where she had photos of the skeletons as they'd initially been found was both frustrating and exhausting.

As each bone was removed from the makeshift grave, it was photographed and numbered, weighed and examined, and then placed on a table until it could be joined with the rest of the bones that would make up an entire human skeleton.

Although they had lights set up in case they wanted to work late, by six o'clock that evening she was ready to call it a day. Her back ached from bending over the burial pit, and her eyes burned from staring at the computer screen for so long.

"Let's go ahead and knock off for the day," she said to Devon.

He nodded and peeled the white lab coat he wore off his broad shoulders and draped it over his chair. "See you in the morning," he said as he left the tent.

She had no idea what Devon did in the evenings. Behind the large lab trailer they had pulled a compact car. Most evenings it was gone, and she assumed that rather than attempt to cook in the small, fairly inadequate kitchenette in the trailer or join the others in the cowboy dining room, he went into town for his evening meals.

Although they had been coworkers for a little over a year now, they didn't share much of their personal lives with each other. She only knew that, like her, he was unmarried and dedicated to his job. That was all she needed to know about him.

She took off her lab coat and slung it across the back of her chair. Her sleeveless white cotton blouse clung to her, and her brown capris felt heavy and hot.

She was just looking forward to a shower and spending a mindless evening indulging in her two secret pleasures: reading tabloids and eating cheese puffs. She also had a stash of protein bars and other nonperishable foods in her room, but cheese puffs were definitely her weakness.

She left the tent and started the long walk to the cowboy motel. At this time of the evening, the ranch was relatively quiet. Most of the men had finished their work for the day and were in the dining room enjoying their dinners.

The grass beneath her feet was slightly crunchy, transforming from the lush spring grass to browning summer-burnt thatch.

The heat would only get worse as summer progressed. Hopefully she could finish up her work here within the next couple of weeks. But bones spoke in their own time, and she knew she couldn't rush things. Rushing resulted in mistakes, and Dr. Patience Forbes didn't make mistakes.

She slowed her pace as the cowboy motel came into view and she saw Forest standing outside his bunk door. Without his hat, his black hair shone shiny and rich in the sunlight and his features were more sharply defined.

Why was he just standing there, as if waiting for her? She'd been abrupt...no, she'd been downright rude when he'd introduced himself to her earlier that day. Why would he want to see or speak to her again?

Maybe he was just waiting for another cowboy to join him to go to dinner. Surely that was it. His handsome, sculptured features transformed into something softer as she drew closer, and he smiled at her.

The warmth of his smile shifted something inside her, heated a place in her stomach she didn't know existed. She didn't like it. She didn't like it at all.

"Good evening," he said.

She nodded and pulled her bunk room key from her back pocket. Before she could put the key into the lock, he lightly touched her forearm and then immediately dropped his hand to his side.

"Dr. Forbes?"

She turned to look at him, struck for the second time that day by the beauty of his bright blue eyes. "Yes?"

"There's a barn dance next Friday night and I was wondering if you'd like to go with me."

"A barn dance?" she parroted in surprise. Was he asking her out for a date? The very thought boggled her mind. She'd certainly given him no indication that she would be remotely open to the possibility of anything like that. "Why would I want to go to a barn dance?" she asked.

He shrugged. "To enjoy the local flavor, to step away from your work for a night of fun…maybe let down your hair a little bit."

"My hair is down and I'm here to work. Thanks, but no thanks." She unlocked her door and stepped inside and closed it behind her.

She immediately sank down on the twin bed, still stunned that he'd actually asked her out. She was thirty years old and the last time a man had asked her out on a date was during her college years, and that had been a huge mistake.

Why on earth would he want to spend any time with her, given the fact that she'd been so...so unlikeable since she'd arrived?

She tossed her key on top of the nearby chest of drawers and then headed for the tiny bathroom where a refreshing shower awaited.

As she stood beneath a tepid spray of water to wash off the dirt and dust of the day, she tried not to think about the handsome cowboy who had asked her out to a barn dance.

Instead she focused on all the reasons she'd chosen to be unlikeable over the course of the years. She'd learned early in her career that being a petite red-haired woman with big green eyes made people doubt her abilities.

She'd had to work twice as hard, twice as long as men in her field to gain the recognition and respect of the people she worked with and for.

She didn't like to be distracted from her work, and a hot, handsome cowboy would definitely be a major distraction. She had no desire for a relationship, so there was no point in being nice or dating. Her snarky attitude kept people at bay and that was the way she liked it.

She got out of the shower, dried off and then pulled a lightweight purple cotton nightshirt over her head. She grabbed a bottle of water from the mini-fridge and a new bag of cheese puffs from her stash of food and then settled on the bed.

She reached beneath the bed and tugged out a plastic bag filled with tabloids. She grabbed one of the slick magazines and opened it to begin to read.

This was how she lived, vicariously through the colorful pictures and outlandish articles about people she didn't know, people she would never meet. It was safe and uncomplicated.

Chapter 2

It was just after noon the next day when Devon drew Patience's attention to the tent door. He stepped outside and she followed him, a slight breeze providing welcome relief from the stifling heat inside the tent.

Devon pointed to where a horse trailer had pulled up to a nearby small corral. "I heard from Adam Benson that a new horse was being delivered today. It's a wild horse that hasn't seen much human contact."

"I didn't know that you and the ranch foreman were so friendly," she replied.

"He's a nice man. I've had dinner with him a couple of times at the café in town."

Patience turned her attention back to the corral. Unlike her, Devon often made nice with the locals when they were working a case.

She recognized Forest as one of the men who got out of the truck that had backed up the trailer to the corral gate. He moved from the front of the truck to the back of the trailer with an unusual grace for a big man and opened the door.

A huge black horse exploded out backward and then bucked and kicked across the corral's arena to the opposite side of the enclosure.

The truck pulled away and Forest closed the corral gate and then rested a foot on the lower rung of the wooden fence and watched the horse.

"The men say he's a horse whisperer," Devon said.

"What does that mean?" she asked, wondering why she cared a bit about what others might say about Forest Stevens.

"It means he has a special touch, that he can communicate with wild horses and work with them to learn to trust human beings. From what I understand, it's a true gift."

"Interesting," she replied and stepped back into the entrance of the tent to get back to work. What was definitely interesting and irritating had been Forest invading her dreams the night before.

Patience almost never dreamed, but when she did, it was either about the case she was working on or a story she'd read in one of her tabloids before going to sleep. She definitely didn't dream about big, hot cowboys with brilliant blue eyes and warm smiles…until last night.

She'd dreamed they'd been at a barn dance, which in and of itself had been odd since she'd never been to such an event in her entire life. Still, they'd been in a barn and there had been music and laughter and he'd held her tight in his big, strong arms as they danced across a hay-strewn floor.

He'd been warm and so intimately close and had smelled of sunshine and wind and fragrant cologne. She'd wanted the dance to never end and then she'd awakened, appalled by what her brain had conjured up for a night fantasy.

She stepped back to the tent doorway and snapped her attention back to the scene before her, where Forest had stepped just inside the corral gate. He looked confident, yet at ease as the horse pawed the ground and eyed him in suspicion.

"Well, I'd love to stand around and watch Forest whisper, but we have work to do. Besides, I'm expecting Chief Bowie to show up sometime soon. I spoke to him this morning and told him we have enough information to indicate that the first victim we've put together from the top of the pit was definitely murdered." Of course the first skeleton they'd pulled from the pit was the last victim of the killer.

Devon nodded and together they returned to the tent and the tedious work at hand. It wasn't long after they'd taken a break for lunch when Chief of Police Dillon Bowie arrived at the entrance of the tent.

Bowie was an attractive man, but he wore the burden of this crime scene in the weary lines of his face and the grim press of his lips.

He paused at the entrance, as if waiting for permission to enter. "You said you have some information for me?"

She motioned him into the tent and to the steel table where a complete human skeleton rested. "We assumed that the people in the pit were probably murder victims. This would have been the last victim of whatever happened here, as we're working from the top of the pit down."

Chief Bowie nodded and stared at the table. "So, what can you tell me about it?"

"Not it, him—the skeleton is that of a young male."

"How young?"

"Between the ages of sixteen and eighteen or so. Thankfully, the teeth are intact in the skull, which helped me with the age issue. I took X-rays and dental impressions so that you could use them to check with dentists, but unfortunately it doesn't look like he'd had any dental work done."

Patience paused to take a breath and then picked up the skull, ignoring the faint distaste that crossed Bowie's features. "This young man was definitely murdered." She turned the skull over to display a long straight crack in the center. "I would guess either a very sharp axe or a meat cleaver, or something like that was used to kill him. I'm leaning toward the meat cleaver due to the narrowness of the injury. It was clean and deep and probably killed him instantly."

She set the skull back on the table. She pointed to another steel table. "As you can see, we're about halfway through putting together the bones to this victim…also male and with the same kind of wound to the back of the skull—and that's all I can give you so far."

Dillon gestured her outside of the hot tent. "Have

you been able to discern how long the bones have been there?"

"As you know when we first arrived on scene, we analyzed soil samples and any insect life present, and of course, the condition of the bones, and my guess would be twelve to sixteen years," she replied. "I'm sorry I can't narrow the time line any better."

His frown deepened. "That means everyone on this ranch and the neighboring ranches are potential suspects."

"I thought you'd already reached that conclusion."

He released a sigh. "I had, but I didn't want to believe it."

"To make your job more complicated, I don't think these people were all killed at the exact same time. The soil samples indicate the first body was buried twelve to fifteen years ago, but the way the bodies were stacked up, I would guess that they were probably killed over the course of a year or so. It wasn't a mass killing that took place all at one time, but rather a serial kind of event. I'll have better clarity about that when we finally get to the bottom of the stack of bones."

He took off his hat and pulled a handkerchief from his pocket. He swiped his forehead and then placed his hat back on his head and tucked the handkerchief away. "This is the first time you've spoken to me without yelling."

A warmth of a blush swept over her cheeks. "My number-one priority is to keep the integrity of the crime scene. I allowed your photographer access to get what photos you needed for your case file, but I'm very proprietary about the scene, especially in the very beginning when something could happen to taint the scene."

"I hadn't noticed," he replied dryly.

She couldn't apologize for doing her job. "If you come back tomorrow, I'll see to it that you have a full report along with the dental records. I'm also bagging any scraps of fabric or hair we find among the bones, although so far there isn't much of either left, and I won't be able to tell you what of those items went with what victim."

"Hopefully, it won't be long before you get to the other bodies?"

"It takes as long as it takes," she replied. She knew he'd been frustrated by how long it had taken her to begin to move the bones from the pit, but there had been much preliminary work that had to be done before actually moving the bones.

There was no way she could pin down a specific time line for him now. She wasn't in control, the bones were. "This is a process that can't be rushed."

He nodded. "Cassie mentioned to me that several times she's invited you to the big house to eat dinner, but you've declined."

"I have," she agreed. "I'm here to work, and generally I don't mix business with pleasure. I prefer to keep myself isolated from the locals. When I'm done with my work, I leave and never look back."

"I just figured I'd mention that Cassie is a terrific woman, just in case you feel inclined to have some girl talk or whatever."

"I'll keep that in mind," Patience replied, although

she had no idea what "girl talk" involved and had no intention of indulging in it. She knew nothing about fashion or shoes or men...or any of the kinds of things she assumed "girl talk" would entail.

"I'll be back sometime in the morning for your report?"

"That's fine," she replied. "I'll make sure I have everything ready on victim one."

She watched as the lawman walked back toward the house, and then her gaze automatically shot to the corral where the big black horse was alone in the enclosure.

She frowned irritably. She'd looked to see if she could catch sight of Forest. What was wrong with her? Why would she even want to look for him? He was just part of the scenery here, nothing more. She returned to the tent and got back to work.

For the next week she focused on the job she was here to do, but found herself at odd times of the day standing in the tent entrance and gazing toward the corral.

Sometimes the horse was there alone and other times Forest was in the corral with the horse. He often stood in one place for a long period of time and then would move, forcing the horse to back away to keep a healthy distance from the human intruder.

Forest appeared to be a patient man, a trait he and Patience shared in common. He didn't attempt to force himself on the huge animal, but appeared to be waiting for the horse to come to him.

By Friday they had managed to piece together all of skeleton two, confirming that it was a young male with the same kind of wound to the back of his skull. She'd written her report, taken the necessary dental X-rays and once again had nothing concrete that would help Dillon Bowie make identification either of the victim or the person responsible for the deaths.

She assumed he was checking missing-persons reports from years ago, but at the time these young men had been murdered, instant technology hadn't been available. He had a difficult task ahead of him, and it was possible the killer was long gone from the area. Of course it was also possible he could be working on this ranch. From what she'd heard, all of the twelve cowboys had been young ranch hands at the time the murders would have taken place.

It was after seven when she and Devon finally knocked off for the day. The officer who showed up each night at around this time to guard the burial scene through the night had already arrived. Even after almost a month, Patience didn't know his name.

He arrived each evening carrying a canvas folding chair that he set up at one end of the tent and settled in for a night of guard duty.

She began the long walk to the cowboy motel. It would be unusually quiet tonight, as Devon had told her most of the cowboys would be headed for the big barn dance being held at Abe Breckinridge's ranch.

She couldn't help but think of Forest's invitation for her to join him at the dance, but her plans were to do what she did every night: eat a protein bar and a prepared salad that Devon had picked up for her at noon when he'd gone into town for a quick lunch. She would then settle in for a night of relaxing and reading Hollywood gossip.

Although her stomach growled with hunger, when she reached her room she opted for a shower first and then changed into her nightshirt. She grabbed both the salad and a soda from the mini-fridge and then got comfortable on the bed to eat.

The silence in the small room didn't bother her; rather, she relished it. Her childhood had been a schizophrenic dichotomy between unexpected outbursts of drama and cold, unemotional lectures.

Since the moment she'd left her parents' home, she'd reveled in the silence of peace. She didn't want anyone else's dramas except her own, and those usually occurred when she allowed her anger free rein.

It was just after nine when the silence was broken. A rousing country Western song drifted through her door along with the distinctive scent of charcoal burning.

What the heck?

She got up off the bed, unlocked her door and peered outside.

Surprise winged through her. Forest was seated in one of two folding chairs just outside his room. The charcoal in the small barbecue grill in front of him glowed red-hot, and as he spied her, he turned down the volume on the CD player next to him.

He was cleaned up, wearing jeans and a pullover short-sleeved blue shirt. His thick black hair was neatly combed and he looked as if he had just shaved. He was way too hot and sexy.

"What are you doing out here?" she asked.

"I figured if you wouldn't go to the barn dance with me, then I'd bring the barn dance to you," he replied and smiled. It was that smile that warmed her in unexpected places as she stared at him in disbelief.

"What do you say? I've got the hot dogs ready for the grill, a couple of beers on ice and the appropriate music. All I'm missing is company."

She should tell him no. This went against all the rules she'd set for herself when she was working. Heck, it went against all the rules she'd set for herself when she wasn't working.

"Just let me pull on something more appropriate and I'll be right out," she heard herself say.

She closed her door and quickly pulled off her nightgown, even while telling herself this was probably a big mistake.

Forest was shocked at her positive response. He'd expected her to say no and then slam her door shut once again. A wave of suspicion swept through him as she disappeared behind her door. Was she really going to get dressed and join him? Or had she vanished back into the room to remain there until he got tired of waiting for her and gave up on the night?

The thin, short-sleeved bright purple nightgown he'd gotten a peek of was incongruent to what he'd imagined she'd wear to bed. He'd spent far too long during the last week wondering about her nightwear.

He'd figured her for a no-nonsense pajama kind of woman, or if it was a nightgown, then it would be long and some muted color like gray or dark blue. He certainly hadn't guessed a short gown that showcased shapely legs and certainly not a brilliant purple that clashed charmingly with her red hair.

Minutes ticked by. This had probably been a hare-brained idea to begin with, he told himself. Still, he'd seen her watching him as he'd started to work with the new horse. Why would she step out of her tent and away from her work so many times during each day to watch him if she didn't have some kind of intrigue about him?

He released a breath he didn't even know he was holding as her door finally reopened and she stepped out into the waning darkness in a pair of black capris and a blue and black sleeveless cotton blouse.

She sank into the chair next to his and shifted positions several times, obviously a bit uncomfortable with the entire situation.

"Cold beer?" he asked.

"Okay," she agreed almost eagerly.

He reached into the nearby cooler and pulled out two beer bottles. He opened hers and handed it to her. "Now, the real question: I've got the grill hot and ready, so how about a hot dog?"

She finally leaned back in the chair. "Is that what they do at barn dances? Drink beer and eat hot dogs?"

"There's definitely a lot of beer and whiskey drinking that goes on, but the menu usually includes smoked ribs and baked beans, tubs of potato salad and all kinds of pies. I couldn't quite accomplish all that so you're stuck with cold beer and hot dogs."

"Then I'll have a hot dog," she replied, again surprising him. His surprise must have shown. "It's only right that I have one since you've gone to so much trouble." She cocked her head to one side and gazed at him. "Why have you gone to all this trouble?"

"I just thought it might do you some good to get out of that room and eat something besides cheese puffs and those dry bars of oats or whatever." He pulled a couple of hot dogs from the cooler and used a fork to set them on the grill.

"How did you know I eat cheese puffs and protein bars?"

"I've seen your trash. It's not healthy for a woman to eat those things on a daily basis without something more substantial." The hot dogs sizzled and filled the air with their scent.

"Actually I had a salad tonight for dinner. Devon picked it up at the café for me at noon." She took a sip of her beer.

"That's good to know." He pulled buns and two squeeze bottles, one of ketchup and of mustard, out of the cooler, along with a couple of paper plates.

Despite the smells of charcoal and cooking meat, he could smell her, a clean scent of minty soap and a faint hint of something floral. His stomach tightened, and he didn't know if it was because he liked the way she smelled or because he'd skipped supper in anticipation of potentially being here with her now.

"What else happens at these barn dances?" she asked curiously.

He turned the hot dogs over before replying. "Music and dancing. There's usually at least one drunken brawl, but rarely any hard feelings afterward." He frowned and thought about the ranch hands who worked the Humes place next to the Holiday Ranch. There didn't have to be booze involved for there to be hard feelings between the cowboys of the two ranches. There was also no reason to bring up that particular unpleasant topic tonight.

"I still don't understand why you did all this. I know what everyone calls me behind my back. I definitely have shown myself to be antisocial and at times downright nasty," she said.

Forest gestured in the direction of the small corral in the distance. "That horse is antisocial, too. But with a lot of patience and a dose of tenderness, he'll wind up being a fine companion." He winced at his own words. "Not that I'm comparing you to a horse."

He busied himself getting the grilled hot dogs to the buns and on the paper plates. She wanted mustard, no ketchup, and he wanted ketchup and no mustard.

"Why didn't you go to the dance with the rest of your friends?" she asked once they each had a plate and he'd tossed two more hot dogs on the grill.

"I was hoping I'd be here with you," he replied easily.

She looked at him as if he had grown two heads. "Why would you want to be here with me?"

He studied her in the light of the full moon that had appeared overhead. Why, indeed? "Beats me," he finally replied honestly. "Why did you agree to come out and sit with me?"

"Beats me," she echoed him.

"To be honest, you've intrigued me since you first arrived here."

"Are you some kind of a masochist? Are you usually drawn to mean women with viper tongues?"

Forest laughed. "None of the above. I'd just like to get to know you a little better, maybe see what's beneath the mean-woman attitude."

"And what if you discover there's only more mean woman underneath?"

He grinned at her. "Then I'll just say it was nice knowing you and won't plan any more barn dances with you." He pulled the other two hot dogs from the grill and was surprised when she agreed to eat another one.

They both fell silent as they ate, but it wasn't an uncomfortable silence. She probably thought he was a nut. She was right. He'd been a little nutty since the first time he'd seen her.

Even before ever talking to her, she'd been in his head as he'd watched her interact, or more accurately, not interact with others. He'd watched the sun spark on her hair whenever she stepped outside of the tent and had wondered if it was as soft to the touch as it looked. He'd wondered what her laughter might sound like, what kind of a person she was when she wasn't working. He'd spent a lot of time wondering all kinds of things about her.

When they'd finished with the hot dogs, he moved the small grill some distance away. The night air was warm enough without the closeness of the heated charcoal. Once he returned to his chair, he turned up the radio, not so loud that they couldn't talk, but so that they could hear the foot-stomping country music.

"I won't ask you about your findings so far, but tell

me a little bit about the work you do as a forensic anthropologist."

"Surely you aren't really interested in that," she protested.

"But I am," he replied. "I only went to school through tenth grade. I'm always interested in learning new things."

The fact that he had so little formal schooling wasn't usually something he talked about, but tragic circumstances and fear had forever changed the path his life was supposed to have taken.

He was interested, but more than that he liked the sound of her voice. When she wasn't screaming or yelling at somebody to get out of her tent, she had a pleasant, almost musical voice that was quite appealing.

He pulled another beer out for each of them and settled back in the chair as she began to talk about soil analysis and the measurement of bone length and density.

Her face came alive when she talked about her work. Her eyes sparkled brightly and her features took on an animation that only made her more attractive than he already found her.

The moonlight lit her hair to a fiery red and bathed her face in an illumination that softened all of her features. By the time she'd finished talking, he wanted more than anything to draw her into his arms and dance with her.

"Facts, that's what I deal in. Scientific facts that never lie," she finished.

"Facts are important, but a little flight of fancy isn't too bad, either," he replied.

She grew silent, and he had a feeling she didn't do flights of fancy often. Instead of discussing the issue, he began to point out the many star constellations that were visible in the night sky and explained how cowboys used the stars to navigate in the dark.

"So, if you ever find a grave of old bones, I'm your girl and if I ever find myself alone in the dark in a pasture, I'd want you by my side," she said.

"I guess that about sums it up," he agreed.

The music had changed to a soft slow rhythm, and on an inward dare to himself, he stood and held out his hand to her. "A barn dance really isn't complete unless you actually dance."

"Oh, I don't know how to dance," she replied and shrank back against the chair.

"It's easy, just follow my lead."

"I'm not used to following anyone's lead," she said with a tiny edge to her voice.

"Jeez, Patience, it's just a simple dance, not a lifetime commitment," he replied.

She hesitated a moment and then set her beer bottle down on the ground. She stood, her body straight and rigid, as if she were being forced to walk a plank to her death.

He took her in his arms, keeping a healthy couple of inches between their bodies. Her hands automatically landed on his upper arms, reminding him of how tiny she was and that reaching up to his shoulders would be a real stretch for her.

"Just relax," he murmured.

She looked up at him. "Easy for you to say."

He laughed and moved his feet in an easy two-step and was pleased to discover that she was a quick study. Within moments she did begin to relax.

The floral scent was more prevalent as he fought the desire to pull her even closer. He knew that if he did, she'd make a hasty retreat back into her room and he wasn't ready for the time with her to end.

It didn't matter what he wanted. The minute the song stopped, she stepped away from him and her body displayed the posture of a deer about to bolt. "I've got to get to bed," she said as she backed up to her door. "This has been pleasant, but it's not something we're going to repeat. I'm here to work and that's all I really care about."

Before Forest could say anything, she disappeared into her room and shut the door after her. Disappointed, he returned to his chair and sank back down, replaying each and every moment of their time together.

He'd half hoped that he'd find her to be as disagreeable as everyone else had deemed her. He'd almost wanted to believe her to be the dragon lady to stanch the inexplicable draw he had to her.

But that hadn't happened. Instead he was more interested in her than he'd been before. His attraction to her was visceral. Perhaps it was just a matter of him suffering a burst of too much testosterone. Maybe he needed to go lift a tree trunk or carry a cow over his shoulders for a couple of miles, he thought wryly.

He unscrewed a fresh beer and looked up at the cloudless starlit sky. No amount of physical activity would relieve the touch of lust that coupled with his desire to get beneath what he suspected was a shell she presented to the world to keep people away.

Forest knew why most of the cowboys working the ranch had trust issues and he had a feeling Dr. Patience Forbes might suffer some trust issues of her own.

Time would tell if she'd be here long enough, if he could get close enough to discover what had made her into the woman she'd become.

All he knew was that as they'd danced and she'd relaxed into him just a bit, she'd touched him in a way nobody but Cass Holiday had when she'd taken him in as a sixteen-year-old runaway who had lost everything. Something about Patience stroked his heart.

Cass was gone now, but Patience was here, and tonight had just whetted his appetite to get closer to her. Although she wasn't a horse, he wondered if he had the magic it might take to allow her to trust him enough to let him get closer to her.

Chapter 3

Patience woke up in a foul mood, and the name of it was Forest Stevens. He'd drawn her out of her comfort zone the night before, enticed her to spend time with him and get to know him a little better.

He'd invaded her dreams with his soft smile and the whole thoughtful setup of a pretend barn dance right outside her door. She'd dreamed of dancing with him closer, more intimately. His strong arms wrapped tight around her, his size making her feel like a tiny dancer in a music box…protected and cherished.

"Foolishness," she said aloud as she dressed for the day. She'd allowed herself to be pulled into his world for a brief moment, a place where she didn't belong, a place she didn't want to belong.

At least the hot dogs had been wonderful, and if she

looked deep inside herself she'd admit that the company had been pleasant enough. Forest Stevens was definitely eye candy with substance.

But acknowledging that didn't change her mood or the fact that she needed to keep her distance from Forest…from everyone and everything except the bones that still awaited her particular expertise.

She left her room, not worried about running into Forest or any of the other cowboys. They would already be up and out, riding the range or doing whatever cowboys did to pass the long days.

Her back stiffened as she drew near the corral and saw Forest inside the wooden enclosure with the horse. He saw her and waved, but she ducked her head and hurried on to the sanctuary of her tent.

She sneaked out only to knock on the trailer door to let Devon know it was time to get to work. He never entered the tent until he knew she was on site. She didn't permit anyone inside unless she was present. She quickly returned to the tent without another glance at the corral.

She didn't even get completely inside the tent when shock stopped her in her tracks. The skeleton they'd completed putting together was gone from the stainless-steel table, as was the second skeleton that had nearly been completed.

For a moment her brain couldn't even begin to make sense of it. Somebody had been inside the tent overnight, somebody who had removed the bones she and Devon had worked so hard to connect into a human form.

Shock turned to outrage. Sensing Devon standing

just behind her, she whirled around to face him. "What happened to the skeletons?"

He looked at her blankly. "What are you talking about?"

"The bones, the skeletons we had on the tables are gone." She was aware of her voice rising not only an octave, but also in volume. "They didn't just get up and walk out of here on their own. Somebody came in here and took them."

Devon backed up several steps and pulled his cell phone from his pocket. "I'll call Dillon."

Devon called Chief Bowie, and Patience paced outside the tent entrance, still stunned by her discovery. She knew better than to enter what now might be a fresh crime scene.

"Dillon said he'll be right here," Devon said as he repocketed his phone. Devon appeared as bewildered and shocked as she felt.

"Who would have done such a thing?" she exclaimed. "And where was the officer who was supposed to be on duty?" Devon shrugged.

She frowned as Forest approached, apparently either seeing her agitated state or hearing her outraged voice. The last thing she needed right now was for the originator of her initial foul mood to interact with her. She already felt as if she was going crazy.

"What's going on?" he asked as he drew closer. He brought with him the scents of leather and sunshine and a faint tinge of soap and fresh-scented cologne.

"My skeletons are missing and it's all your fault," she said angrily.

"My fault?" He raised a dark brow in apparent confusion.

"You distracted me last night with your barn dance. You…you made me not think about the bones and my work here." In the back of her head she knew she was being completely irrational, but she was angry and confused and he was the nearest target.

She couldn't very well yell at Devon. She had to work closely with him for who knew how long. Besides, he got the sharp end of her tongue on most days.

"And if I hadn't distracted you last night what would be different this morning?" Forest asked in a calm, even tone.

She stared at him for a long tense minute. "Nothing," she finally admitted. With that admission her anger shifted into a weary confusion.

If she hadn't sat outside with him for his makeshift barn dance, she would have been in her room all night and still wouldn't have answers as to what had happened to her skeletons.

"At least I got the reports on the first skeletal remains to Dillon already," she said more to herself than to Forest or Devon. "Why would somebody do this? What could be their possible motivation?"

"To stop or slow down the process? Maybe to prevent you from finding something that might identify either the victims or the killer?" Forest replied. "I thought there was somebody on guard duty here during the night hours."

"There is supposed to be," she replied. "He comes around between six and seven at night and stays until about seven in the morning. I'm sure he was here on duty last night before I knocked off work for the night." She glanced at her watch. It was a few minutes after eight. He'd already left for the day.

She sank down to the ground, unmindful of the dusty reddish earth beneath her butt. To her surprise, Forest sat down next to her.

"I'm sorry I yelled at you," she said as Devon returned to the trailer and went inside to await Dillon's arrival.

"You were upset," Forest replied.

"I'm still upset, but it's not your fault. All the work we've accomplished since we arrived is gone. Almost a month's worth of digging, testing, matching and re-creating skeletons from a jumble of bones is now all for nothing. Nothing like this has ever happened to me before at any site I've ever worked."

She was surprised to discover a lump in the back of her throat and the burn of tears in her eyes. Surely she wasn't about to cry. She didn't cry. It implied weakness and crying had never been allowed.

Swallowing against the lump and mentally willing away the alien tears, she was grateful to see Dillon Bowie's patrol car pull up next to the big ranch house and park.

Both she and Forest got to their feet as the chief of police hurried toward them. "Maybe he'll be able to figure this out," Forest said with a touch of optimism.

Patience wished she could steal some of that hopeful outlook from him. She was still defaulting to a rich anger that had felt safe and familiar for so long.

"I thought somebody was on guard duty during the

nights. What happened to your officer last night? Did he leave for pizza or take a nap or just forget what he was here for last night?" she asked when Dillon joined them.

Dillon winced at the same time Forest lightly touched her shoulder. "He's not your enemy, either," Forest said softly.

Heat filled Patience's cheeks and she drew in a deep, steadying breath. "I'm sorry," she said, wondering how many times she would find herself apologizing for her temper before the day was over.

Didn't either man understand how this would set them back? She hadn't even been inside the tent to see if bones from the burial site were also missing. If they were, then the odds of solving this crime were zero. Evidentiary chain of command would have been broken, and she couldn't analyze what was no longer present.

"Officer Kelly was on duty last night. I spoke to him right after Dr. Lewison called me. He confessed to me that he fell asleep for about an hour."

"Fell asleep for about an hour," Patience parroted in frustration. "Does he have any idea how important the work we're doing here is? That this is a site filled with victims of foul play? This is a crime scene and it has to be guarded at all times. People can't take naps when on duty."

"He does understand all that and he'll be appropriately reprimanded," Dillon replied evenly. "Have you been inside?" He gestured toward the tent.

"No, when I stepped to the doorway I saw that the skeletons were missing," she replied. "I figured it was officially a new crime scene and so I haven't been all the way inside."

"Where's Dr. Lewison?" Dillon asked.

"In the trailer." Patience walked over to the huge vehicle and knocked on the door. Devon stepped out and they rejoined Dillon and Forest.

"I'm assuming you didn't hear anything odd or disturbing overnight?" Dillon asked Devon.

Devon shook his head. "I work hard and I sleep hard." The short, well-built man raked a hand through his brown hair. He punched the center of his dark-rimmed glasses to settle them properly on the bridge of his nose. "I didn't hear a thing."

"Let's take a look inside and see exactly what we're dealing with," Dillon said. "Nobody touch anything," he cautioned them.

There was no point in wearing booties, as the floor in the tent was hard earth that didn't retain footprints. Dillon entered first, followed by Patience, then Devon and finally Forest.

She was vaguely surprised that Forest hadn't returned to his work in the corral once Dillon had arrived. He wasn't needed here and couldn't add anything to help solve the mystery. She found his continued presence both a faint irritation and a strange comfort.

She knew this scene was important to Dillon, who had to investigate the circumstances as to how these people were killed and buried. But Forest knew how important her work was to her after their little bonding session the night before. He would understand why she was so upset.

"The skeletons are gone," Dillon stated the obvious as he stared at the two empty tables. A deep frown cut across his forehead.

Patience fought the impulse to roll her eyes. "Just as I told you," she replied as evenly as possible. She walked over to the burial pit to see if any or all the other bones had been stolen from there.

She gasped in surprise as she saw that the bones that had been on the tables were not missing, but rather had been tossed back in with the others in the pit. She'd numbered each one and the numbered bones were there.

"They're here," she said. All three men moved to stand beside her and peer down. "Thank goodness part of the process is to number the bones as I put them in place. I see both number-one and number-two on the bones on top. Those are the ones that had been on the tables."

"Are they all there?" Dillon asked. Forest stood next to him, tall and steady as a big oak tree.

"It's hard to tell without actually pulling them out and reconstructing the skeletons," she replied.

"So, this isn't a theft, it's a case of criminal mischief," Dillon said with a trace of anger deepening his voice.

"It would appear so," Devon muttered.

"What bothers me is that somebody had to have been watching Officer Kelly, waiting and hoping that he might nod off so that the culprit could enter the tent," Forest said. "It wasn't a spur-of-the-moment decision, but rather a planned bit of mischief or whatever."

"And why go to all the bother of doing this?" Devon

asked. "If the bones in the pit had been stolen, we would have had a real problem; as it is we've just been set back a bit."

"Depending on what time Officer Kelly fell asleep, it's doubtful there were any witnesses around. I think all of the men went to the barn dance last night and they wouldn't have gotten back here until late," Forest added. "Even then most of them wouldn't have been in any condition to notice anyone lurking around in the tent."

"I'll round up all the men anyway and find out if anyone saw anything," Dillon said. "How long will it take you to get back on track?" He looked at Patience.

"It will probably take us two days or so to redo what we'd already had done," she replied. "And that's only if all the bones are actually there."

"I doubt if it would do any good to try to fingerprint either the table or the bones." Dillon shoved his hands in his pockets, frustration lacing his voice. "Whoever was smart enough to wait for my officer to fall asleep, probably was also smart enough to wear gloves."

"Besides, fingerprinting the bones isn't a good idea, as it might degrade what's already so fragile," Patience replied.

Dillon motioned them outside of the tent. He looked at Devon and Patience. "You two have your work cut out for you, and I'll be asking questions around here for most of the day."

He didn't wait for a reply but turned around and headed for the big house where Patience assumed he'd update the owner of the ranch, Cassie, on this latest development.

Forest gazed at her. "Are you all right?"

She straightened her back. "Of course. I'm fine. I just need to get to work." In truth, a sense of violation filled her. It was as if somebody had rifled through her underwear drawer. Not that it would give anyone any thrills...just basic white cotton. But she didn't want him to know how shaken up she was concerning this whole thing.

Forest tipped his black hat and then began his walk back to the corral where he'd been working when she'd first gone ballistic. She watched him go and remembered her dream, when she'd been held in his big, strong arms.

For a brief moment she wished she could call him back and meld into his arms. It was such a shocking thought, she turned to Devon. "Let's get to work," she said briskly and shoved all thoughts of Forest out of her head.

If Forest had hoped that the barn dance he'd orchestrated or his silent support of Patience when she'd discovered her bones had been moved would prompt some sort of forward momentum in their friendship, then he was mistaken.

For the past week she'd been as skittish as the horse he'd been working with, where he was concerned. She worked in the tent throughout the day and then surprisingly, she'd driven off with Devon at dinner time, presumably to eat at the local café.

At night he never heard her return to her room, and it was obvious she was avoiding him. Still, even as he'd worked each day with the horse in the nearby corral, she'd often stepped outside the tent and watched him. He might be crazy, but he wasn't willing to give up on her yet.

Although he admitted that he had a healthy dose of lust where she was concerned, he also thought she just might need a friend, and if that's all that he could have of her, he'd gladly take it.

Just as he knew the horse wanted to trust, he sensed that Patience yearned for some connection, but it could just be the imagining of a lonely cowboy.

He'd heard through the grapevine that Dillon's investigation as to who had moved the bones had gone nowhere. Forest definitely didn't want to believe that any of the men he'd lived and worked with for the past fifteen years or so could be responsible.

But who? And why?

Twilight was falling and he sat in a chair just outside his room. He glanced over to where the Humes ranch met Holiday land. Nobody knew what had initially caused the friction between Raymond Humes and Cass Holiday, but there was no question that there was bad blood between the two ranches and their workers.

The Holiday Ranch had suffered downed fences, small fires and damage to outbuildings, and Forest and his fellow cowboys suspected the culprits came from right next door.

Raymond Humes had hired thugs and bullies for ranch hands and many of them had worked for the man for the near sixteen years that Forest had worked on the Holiday Ranch.

Was one of them a killer?

Or had the killer been a drifter who had spent time in Bitterroot or on some other ranch years ago and was now far away from Oklahoma?

"Why are you sitting out here all alone?" Sawyer Quincy sat in the second chair that Forest had dragged out of his room in hopes of getting Patience to sit and chat with him when she got home from wherever she and Devon had gone.

"Just sitting," Forest replied.

"Looks to me like you're sitting and waiting." Sawyer's russet-colored hair looked more gold than red as the sun sank lower in the sky. "You've got two chairs out here so it's obvious you're waiting for somebody, and I suspect it's a red-headed firecracker."

Forest didn't reply.

"I know you, Forest. Of all of us you're the one most likely to want marriage and family, but you aren't going to find it with Dr. Forbes."

Forest laughed. "I'm not looking for anything from Patience. I just think she could use a friend around here." Somewhere in the back of his mind he wondered exactly when she'd become Patience instead of Dr. Forbes.

"She doesn't act like she wants or needs a friend," Sawyer replied.

"Everybody needs somebody," Forest said. "Where would all of us have been without Cass, without each other?"

Sawyer's eyes darkened. "I don't even want to think about it. How do you know Dr. Forbes doesn't already have somebody in her life? Maybe some hot, handsome scientist-type back in Oklahoma City?"

Forest was surprised by a momentary skip of his heartbeat. He leaned back in his chair and drew in a deep breath. He hadn't thought of her already having somebody important in her life. Maybe that was why she was so determined to keep him and everyone else here at a distance.

He should have realized that a woman as educated, as accomplished and as pretty as Patience would have a man important to her in her life.

"I just don't want to see a big man with a big heart take a hard fall," Sawyer said. He got up from the chair. "I'll see you around in the morning." Sawyer walked past several rooms and then disappeared into his own.

Forest sat forward in his chair to digest what Sawyer had said. Did Patience have a significant somebody in Oklahoma City? Was that the reason she'd kept herself so isolated from everyone? Because she had some special man waiting for her back home?

If that was the case, then Forest would stop his subtle pursuit of her. He would never try to come between a couple even if they were just casually dating. It was a matter of honor…honor that had been instilled in him first by his parents and then by Cass.

While he appreciated Sawyer's concern for him, Forest didn't take the chairs and go back inside. Instead he continued to sit and wait, not knowing what might happen or what he might learn when she returned.

It was nearly dark when he saw headlights that indicated Devon and Patience had returned from wherever they had gone. Forest's heart stepped up its rhythm just a bit as the car lights went out.

He'd wanted to talk to her, but now with Sawyer's questions ringing in his ears, he wanted to talk to her more than ever. It would be difficult for her to avoid him given the fact he was seated just to the side of her room door.

Of course she could always fly by him with a curt nod of her head and escape into her room without having any conversation with him, as she had done all week long.

He sat up straighter when she approached, a mere silhouette swinging a white plastic bag as she walked in the moonlight. He could tell the moment she saw him. The bag stopped swinging and her shoulders punched back in a defensive mode.

It was definitely not a happy-to-see-you kind of posture. As she drew close enough to see her features, he relaxed a bit. Her lips weren't pressed together in displeasure, nor were her eyes narrowed in a glare.

"Want to sit for a few minutes?" he asked when she got close enough.

She stepped up to her door and hesitated a moment. "Okay," she finally said. "Let me just put my bag inside." She unlocked her door and tossed the bag in the direction of where Forest knew her bed was located.

"More cheese puffs and tabloids?" he asked.

"You've got to stop looking at my trash," she replied as she sat in the chair next to his.

"Can't help it. Once a week it's my chore to empty all the trash cans everyone puts outside their doors. At least your trash is more interesting than the usual beer bottles and beef jerky wrappings. I can't believe you read those tabloids."

"I like them. I read about people with interesting lifestyles that have nothing in common with mine."

"Wouldn't it be better to just find somebody like that and talk to them? Get to know them on a personal level?" he asked.

"Not really. I don't do emotional attachments and I don't have to worry about that with the stories I read."

"So, there's no boyfriend or significant other waiting for you to return to Oklahoma City?" he asked, hoping he sounded nonchalant.

"Absolutely not. I dated a bit in college, but I came to the conclusion that I don't really believe in love. It's just a bunch of messy emotions that aren't fact based. It's something people do to procreate and not be alone as they get older and I don't mind being alone."

Forest stared at her in shock. "Not everything in life is fact based, especially when it comes to matters of the heart. How do you explain people who stay married for years?"

"A chemical attraction based on pheromones, evolution, need and hormones. In the lust and attraction stage dopamine and adrenaline play a big part. In the attachment stage the hormones oxytocin and vasopressin kick in. It's science, Forest, not the nebulous emotion people call love."

Forest had never heard of half the words she'd spoken, but he got the gist of what she was communicating and it made him sad for her.

"I don't know anything about hormones and evolution, but until I was fifteen I was raised by my mother and father who not only loved each other but also loved me. I just don't believe science had anything to do with it. It was an emotional, loving bond that was only broken by death."

"Your parents died?"

"In a car accident when I was fifteen." Even after all the years that had passed, a lump of loss rose in his throat. "What about you? Are your parents still alive and well?"

"My mother also died in a car accident. It was five years after she walked out on me and my father. She left us when I was six and we never heard from her again. My father was contacted when she died by a distant relative of hers."

"I'm sorry," he replied.

"Don't be. She was a drama queen, constantly wailing or crying, cursing and screaming. I think if she hadn't left when she did, my father might have divorced her. He couldn't abide the chaos of all of her emotions." She spoke matter-of-factly, as if relating one of the stories in her tabloids about people she didn't know well.

"Do you have a good relationship with your father?" Forest was fascinated by this glimpse into her childhood.

"We have a good working relationship," she replied.

Forest frowned. "What does that mean?"

"My father is a scientist and we've never had a warm and fuzzy relationship. He was my mentor and set high standards for me. We speak occasionally on the phone, but he lectures a lot all over the country, so we don't see each other very often." She shifted positions in the chair, the movement sending her faint floral scent to Forest. "What happened to you after your parents' deaths? Did you go into foster care?"

"We lived in Oklahoma City and after my parents' funeral I was taken back to my house by a social worker. I packed a duffel bag and crawled out of my bedroom window and took to the streets. I wasn't going to go into foster care. I thought I was old enough, big enough to take care of myself. On the streets is where I first met Dusty."

"Dusty?"

"Blond hair, deep dimples…the youngest of all of us here. He was a scrawny thirteen-year-old who was getting beat up and robbed on a regular basis by other street kids. I was already big enough that nobody messed with me. After I met Dusty I made sure nobody ever messed with him again."

"How did you come to be on a ranch an hour and a half from the city?"

"A woman named Francine Rogers. She was a social worker who at night would check in with the lost boys…that's what we called ourselves. At the time I met her, Cass had just lost her husband and this ranch was in near ruins. Hank, Cass's husband, had been ill for some time and most of the men who worked the ranch had moved on and deserted her. Francine asked me if I wanted to come here and learn to be a cowboy. I agreed only if Dusty came with me, and here we are roughly fifteen years later. All of us were street kids when Cass took us in and turned us into men."

"You know the timing is right that it's possible one of those street kids committed murder."

"I'll never believe that," he replied firmly. "I'll definitely have to see cold, hard facts to believe that."

"See, I guess we're more alike than you want to admit." She stood. "And on that note, I'm going inside. Good night, Forest."

"'Night, Patience," he replied.

When she'd disappeared into her room, he leaned back in his chair, digesting everything they'd talked about. Forest had no idea who might have killed the people whose bones Patience was attempting to put together, but if he was to guess, it might have something to do with the feud between Raymond and Cass.

He wasn't a police officer and it wasn't his job even to speculate on who might be responsible. What he'd found intriguing about his conversation with Patience was the glimpses into her childhood…a childhood that had made her into the woman she was today.

Raised for six years by an over-emotional mother who had abandoned her and then brought up by what sounded like a cold and distant scientist father, was it any wonder she questioned the existence of real love?

Was it any wonder her only emotion appeared to be a default to anger, the easiest of all emotions to attain and the best weapon to keep other people and more frightening emotions away?

Forest knew the sounds, the scents and the feel of love. Love sounded like his mother and father laughing as they shared a private joke between them. Love smelled like pot roast on Sundays, and it felt like a proud pat on the back or a gentle kiss on the cheek just before falling asleep.

He knew love and he hungered to have it in his life again. Unlike most of the other men who worked here, Forest hadn't been beaten or abused by the people who were supposed to love him or damaged on the streets where he'd found himself.

He wanted love and marriage, children and the kind of forever after he knew in his heart his mother and father would have shared if they hadn't died prematurely.

He rose from the chair and folded it and the second one where Patience had sat and carried them inside his room. He locked his door and tried not to imagine Patience in her bed just on the other side of the wall of his room.

It was just his luck that the first woman who had captured his attention didn't believe in love and had no interest in personal relationships.

He shucked off his jeans and took off his shirt, leaving him clad only in a pair of navy boxers. He got into bed and wondered if it was even possible for him to change Patience's mind about the most important things in life.

Chapter 4

Cassie greeted Dillon at the door of the large, two-story ranch house and led him into the kitchen where foreman Adam Benson sat at the table with a cup of coffee before him.

"'Morning, Adam," he said to the handsome, dark-haired man.

"Same to you," Adam replied.

"Coffee?" Cassie asked.

"Sounds good," Dillon agreed. Cassie Peterson was a petite sexy blonde, who had attracted Dillon from the day he'd first met her when she'd arrived at the ranch after her aunt's death.

But it had become quickly obvious to him that Adam and Cassie were close and becoming closer with each day that passed, so he'd tamped down his initial interest in her.

That didn't stop him from admiring the way her designer jeans fit snug across her shapely butt and clung to her slender legs. It didn't stop him from noticing how the light blue blouse she wore enhanced the sky color of her eyes.

He sat at the table across from Adam, and she placed a cup of coffee before him and then sat between the two men. "I thought I'd give you an update and ask you a few questions."

She raised a perfectly formed blond eyebrow. "Questions for me? If it is about those skeletons, then I won't have any answers for you. You know I've only been on the ranch a couple of months."

"I do, but let me tell you what we've learned and the theory I'm working with. Both of the skeletons that Dr. Forbes has managed to put together are of young males." He looked at Adam. "They would have been about the same age all of you cowboys were when you first arrived at the ranch."

Adam frowned. "I was the first street kid that Cass took in. I was here at the very beginning and I don't remember anyone else being brought here except the twelve of us who have always been here."

Dillon looked back at Cassie. "Are there records from when Cass first began to bring the young men to the ranch?"

Cassie glanced at Adam and then back at Dillon. "I wouldn't even begin to know where to look."

"I might have something," Adam said. "There are

boxes of ranch bookkeeping records in one of the sheds. Of course now we keep computer records, but that didn't happen until a couple of years ago. Cass was old-fashioned and didn't like new technology. I had to practically beg her to let me start using a computer."

"Can you go through those old papers and see if you can locate employment records for the first two or three years that Cass hired on all of you?" Dillon asked.

"Sure, but I doubt if you'll find them too helpful. I'm not sure if every cowboy working here used their real legal names when they first started working for Cass. I'm definitely sure that none of us had addresses. Cass pretty much relied on Francine to bring her young men she thought would work well on the ranch. Have you contacted Francine?"

"I've tried to. She retired several years ago and moved from Oklahoma City to Tulsa. I spoke to an old friend of hers who told me Francine is currently on a Mediterranean cruise and won't be home for another two weeks." Dillon took a big drink of his coffee.

"And I've already checked on all of you working here. Everyone used their legal names and I ran background checks on all of you," Dillon said.

Adam raised an eyebrow. "I'm assuming those background checks came out clean." Dillon nodded. "Are you doing the same kind of investigation into the men working the Humes ranch?"

"In the process of doing so now," Dillon replied.

"Maybe by then Dr. Forbes will have all the skeletons put together and the scene here can be shut down," Cassie said hopefully. "Seeing that blue tent on the property makes me sick to my stomach every time I look at it."

"We all feel that same way," Adam replied. "Do you have any potential suspects? Any real clues that might lead you to who is responsible for such a thing?"

"I really can't give specific details about an ongoing investigation," Dillon replied. He finished his coffee and stood. "If either of you could find me any kind of employment records from the time in question, let me know. Cassie, don't get up. I can see myself out."

"Adam and I will see what we can find," Cassie replied.

Dillon nodded and then left the kitchen. He walked through the large great room and into a smaller formal parlor and then out the front door.

He got into his patrol car and sat for a length of time before starting the engine. He'd love to be able to share specifics of leads with somebody, but the truth was he didn't have any real leads.

Dr. Forbes had indicated that her best guess about the wounds to each of the skulls was that the weapon used was a meat cleaver.

Dillon had already had a discussion with Cookie, the cook for the Holiday cowboys, and asked him about his meat cleavers. Cookie, aka Cord Cully, was a curmudgeon to the nth degree and hadn't been particularly pleasant to talk to, but he had been forthcoming in that over the years he'd thrown half a dozen meat cleavers away to get new, better ones.

He'd shown Dillon what cleavers he possessed, each

one clean and wickedly sharp and obviously not what was used so many years ago to kill six people.

Dillon had run a background check on the man who had worked for Cass for twenty years. She'd hired him when he was thirty-five to cook for the ranch hands who had eventually abandoned the ranch when Cass's husband had gotten ill. Cord had had a few run-ins with the law when he'd been younger, mostly bar fights and minor offenses, but nothing that had raised Dillon's suspicions about him to a new level.

Dillon finally started his car, turned around and headed down the long road leading to the highway that would take him back to his office in Bitterroot.

He'd spoken at length with former Chief of Police Ralph McCrillis, who had been chief at the time that the murders might have occurred.

Ralph had no information about missing young men, murder or anything else that had taken place on the Holiday Ranch so many years ago.

It was a logical theory to work from that these young men had arrived at the Holiday Ranch the same way the other cowboys who worked there now had. But who had killed them? Who had sneaked up behind each one of them and hit them in the back of the skull with a meat cleaver?

Who had buried them in the hole beneath the old shed? And why?

He could only hope that when Francine Rogers got back from her cruise he could have a sit-down with her. He especially hoped she had kept some kind of re-cords as to the identities of the young men she'd taken off the street and brought to her good friend Cass to help work the ranch. But it had been a long time ago, and he couldn't help but feel pessimistic about the case.

Memories would have faded and it was possible the dead would never be identified and the killer never found, and if that was the case, then he would be haunted for the rest of his life.

The third skeleton was coming together more easily than the first two, and Patience was pleased to discover that the skull held a gold crown, which meant that someplace there might be dental records for this particular victim.

Although she was aware that because the murders had occurred about fifteen years or so ago, finding those dental records without a name to go with them would probably be fruitless. It was something new for Dillon to work with.

The work was going smoothly, but she was irritated with herself for succumbing to Forest's invitation to sit with him for a while the night before.

She'd told him too much. She'd given away little pieces of her past that she had never shared with anyone. He just made it so easy to talk to him, to trust that anything she told him was safe.

Time and time again today she'd fought the impulse to step out of the tent and watch his work in the corral with the horse, but so far she'd successfully fought her temptation.

The big man appeared to have an easy way and a soft heart that made her brain scream that he was dangerous to her, and yet there was no question that she was drawn to him as she'd never been to a man before.

Her one and only foray into romance had taken place in college. His name had been Jason and they'd only dated three times. It had been after their third date that she had given him her virginity only to find out later that she had been part of a bet between Jason and a bunch of his frat house buddies.

The bet was that Jason couldn't get the brainiac red-head into bed. Patience had lost her virginity and her trust in men and Jason had garnered a big pay day for his seduction success.

Rationally she knew that all men weren't Jasons, but she'd never dated after that. She'd focused solely on her studies, graduated from college almost two years early and wound up finishing her doctorate by the age of twenty-eight.

Work she knew. She trusted in her intelligence and her job. Even though something about Forest touched her, she couldn't lose sight of the fact that when she was finished here she would be returning to her apartment in Oklahoma City.

The unidentified bones might haunt her, as might her fascination with a broad-shouldered cowboy, but there would be another job to work, more bones to process and her life would go on.

It was after six when she told Devon he could knock off for the night. "Do you want to ride with me into town for dinner?" he asked.

"No, I'm going to work a while longer here and then head to my room," she replied.

She knew Devon didn't particularly enjoy dining with her and would much prefer sharing his dinner with some of the locals.

Besides, she intended to work to finish the third skeleton before bedtime and that would take several more hours. It had taken so long to prepare the scene and document everything before actually beginning the work of excavation. She was eager to continue the work of actually putting bones together again.

Hopefully it would be late enough when she returned to her room that if Forest was waiting for her she could simply say she was exhausted.

She'd never had a problem before talking sharply, being demanding and keeping people at bay. But for some reason she didn't want to hurt Forest's feelings.

She shoved away all thoughts of Forest and her past and instead returned to the tedious work. The human skeleton contained two hundred and six bones, and at the moment, skeleton three had one hundred and ninety on the table. Finding and matching the final sixteen bones would take complete focus on her part.

She worked for a couple of hours and then as twilight moved in she sat and drank a soda and dug into her stash of cheese puffs. She was still missing six bones to complete the skeleton.

Devon had returned from town a little while before. He'd poked his head into the tent to see if she wanted his help, but she'd told him to relax in the trailer until morning. He'd also told her the guard had arrived for the night and had set up for duty on the side of the tent.

While she munched, her thoughts returned to Forest and the conversation they'd shared the night before. With his size and muscular build, it was no wonder he hadn't had problems living on the streets. The fact that he'd taken a vulnerable younger Dusty under his wing only spoke to the bigness of Forest's heart.

But he believed in the kind of nebulous things she didn't, like love and fairy tales. He probably even believed in pixies and Santa Claus.

With a frown she finished her soda and stashed her bag of cheese puffs back into the cooler and then returned to work. Discerning which bone went with each body was a challenge, but using length and color, weight and sameness of bones helped her figure out which belonged to the particular skeleton she was working on and which didn't.

It was after ten when she finally placed the last bone, a metacarpal in the hand, to complete skeleton number three. She stared at the finished product and then used her laptop to make notes.

This particular skeleton not only had the skull wound of the others, but also displayed signs of an arm broken in two places and a fractured shoulder.

These poor old bones had been abused long before the person was killed. The injuries appeared to have happened in childhood, although they had been healed fully at the time of death.

Was this another runaway who had been brought to the ranch to work for Cass? Had he run to escape abuse only to be brought here to his death?

She left the tent and began the long walk to the sprawling cowboy motel in the distance. She didn't envy Dillon in his quest to solve this case. Sometimes it took years and years to identify the dead and even longer to identify a killer.

Thick clouds danced across the light of the three-quarter moon, making the walk even darker than usual. A whisper of sound on the grass behind her gave her a sudden sense of strange vulnerability.

She whirled around, but saw nothing in the darkness behind her. She released a sigh of relief and picked up her pace, eager to get into the safety of her room, even though she had no reason to feel afraid.

She was about twenty feet away from her room when she sensed somebody behind her, a crunch of dried grass, a creepy-crawly skitter up her spine. Before she could turn around to see if anyone was there, a blow landed on the back of her head.

Stars shot off in her vision as incredible pain exploded in her skull. She managed to scream just once before she fell to her knees and crashed to the ground in total blankness.

The scream was barely audible, but shot Forest off his bed. He yanked on a pair of jeans and a T-shirt, grabbed his gun and burst out of his room with a rush of adrenaline.

He was vaguely aware of other ranch hands exiting their rooms, guns out and ready for whatever actions might be necessary.

He froze just outside the door, allowing his eyes to adjust from the brightness of his room to the darkness of the night. He listened intently, but heard nothing except the sound of crickets and other night insects singing their songs.

He didn't see anyone in the dark, but he would swear he'd heard a sharp, short scream, and it was obvious by the others who had left their rooms that they had heard something, too.

"Spread out and check the grounds," Forest yelled to the others. At the same time he banged on Patience's door, the loud knocks also resounding in his heart. The scream had definitely been female.

When there was no reply from Patience, he banged on the door again. Nothing happened and he knew she wasn't in her room. His heartbeat accelerated and he hurried in the direction of the dark tent, using the general path she always took from there to her room.

Officer Ben Taylor came running from the tent area, along with Devon who had apparently left the trailer. "What happened? I heard somebody scream, but I was on the other side of the tent and didn't see anyone," Ben said.

"It was Patience," Forest said and then nearly stumbled over her prone body on the ground. "Here, she's here," he cried to the others as he knelt down beside her.

"Patience?" She was facedown, with her head turned to one side. "Patience," he said again even though it was obvious she was unconscious.

Dusty and Sawyer raced to Forest. "Get me a car, I need to get her to the hospital," Forest said frantically. There was no way he was waiting for an ambulance from town to arrive and then take her back to the hospital. She needed medical attention as soon as possible.

"Are you sure you should move her?" Dusty asked worriedly. He flicked on a flashlight and shone it on her.

"I can't wait around for old Doc Washington or an ambulance to get out here. She needs help right now." She looked so tiny, so lifeless and pale, and he had no idea why she had screamed and was now on the ground unconscious. What had happened to her between the tent and her room?

By that time Sawyer pulled up in the car that had once belonged to Cass, a vehicle that was always ready not only for Cassie to use, but for the ranch hands who might need it for one thing or another.

Sawyer remained in the driver seat. Forest hesitated only a moment, Dusty's concerns ringing in his ears. Would moving her make things worse? He didn't see any obvious broken bones, but he also wasn't a doctor.

She certainly wasn't going to get any help with him being too concerned, too hesitant to act. He shoved his gun in the back of his waistband and then as gently as possible, he picked her up in his arms.

Light as a feather and still not showing any sign of waking, she lay limp in his arms as he placed her into the backseat and he crawled in next to her and placed her head in his lap.

Fear rode with him as Sawyer tore out of the ranch entrance. Had she fainted? He knew she'd been living mostly on junk food and sodas. He should have insisted she join the cowboys in the dining room where she could eat healthy, hardy meals each evening.

"Patience, can you wake up?" He stroked a finger down the side of her cheek. Soft, her skin was so soft.

But the longer she remained unresponsive the more worried he grew.

The only thing that gave him some modicum of relief was that her breathing appeared normal. There was no bruising on her face, no indication that she'd hit her forehead on the ground. She just looked like she was asleep. They had just turned into the Bitterroot Hospital when she regained consciousness.

She looked up at Forest and frowned. "What happened?" She struggled to sit up, but Forest held her down. "Where am I?" Her eyes radiated sheer panic.

"Patience, everything is all right now. We're at the hospital. You've been unconscious," he replied, grateful as Sawyer pulled to the Emergency entrance.

"What happened?" she repeated.

"We don't know yet."

Sawyer pulled to a stop, got out of the car and raced for the entrance. He appeared a moment later with two orderlies maneuvering a gurney toward the car.

"What happened?" Patience repeated yet again, increasing Forest's concern. "I think I'm going to throw up."

Forest got her out of the car just in time for her to bend over and puke. Forest held on to her and once she was finished, she was placed on the gurney. "We found her unconscious on the ground," Forest said. One of the orderlies nodded and she was quickly whisked away.

"Go to the waiting room," one of the men yelled over his shoulder.

Inside the building, Sawyer sat on one of the padded chairs, and Forest paced, his heart still beating too fast as he tried to figure out what had happened to her.

Had she merely tripped over the uneven ground? It just didn't seem possible that she'd fallen forward and hit her head hard enough to render her unconscious, especially since there had been no marks on her forehead or anywhere on her lovely face.

"I hope the rest of the men checked out the area where she was," Sawyer said. "If somebody attacked her, then maybe they found something that might help us find the person."

Forest threw himself in the chair next to his buddy. His worry transformed into a simmering rage. "If somebody attacked her, then Dillon better figure out who it was and let me know the name."

"I'd hate to have to visit you in prison," Sawyer said dryly.

"I won't kill him, but I'll make damn sure he wishes I did," Forest said with fervor. "Besides, until we hear from the doctor or Patience, we probably shouldn't jump to any conclusions."

Still as they waited it was difficult not to jump to all kinds of crazy conclusions. Had she been bitten by a snake? Had she fainted from exhaustion? Then why did she scream?

Something had obviously frightened her for her to scream. What on earth had happened in the dark of night that might have rendered her unconscious?

His momentary rage went back to full-blown worry as the agonizing wait continued. He finally got up and began to pace once again, unable to sit still as concern jumped and bubbled inside him.

Finally Dr. Clayton Rivers came out to speak to them. Clayton was thirty years old, two years younger than Forest. The two had socialized at town events over the years.

"First of all, she's going to be all right," he said before Forest or Sawyer could speak.

A rush of sweet relief washed over Forest. "What's wrong with her?" he asked.

"She shows all the symptoms of a mild to moderate concussion, so I took some X-rays. She has a goose egg on the left side of the back of her head, and I'd say she was whacked with some blunt object. She remembers nothing of the event, but that's not unusual in the case of a concussion."

"But she's going to be okay?" Forest asked worriedly, tamping down his outrage at the idea of somebody sneaking up behind her and hitting her over the head. He'd deal with that particular emotion later.

"She should be fine. I'd like to keep her here tonight under observation, but she's refusing quite firmly and quite colorfully to stay."

"Then she must be okay," Sawyer muttered under his breath.

"I can't force her to remain here," Clayton said. "She's already told me several times that she'll leave against medical advice."

Forest released a deep sigh. He knew if she had made up her muddled mind, then nothing and nobody would change it. "If we take her back to the ranch, what needs to be done for her?"

Clayton frowned. "First and foremost she needs bed rest. She needs to relax and not strain her brain for the next couple of days. I don't want her left alone for tonight. Somebody needs to sit with her to make sure her symptoms don't get worse. I know it's a little old school, but she needs to be awakened about every hour or so and her pupils checked to make sure they stay the same size and shape. If things change, if she throws up or shows more confusion, then she needs to be brought back here immediately."

"I'll take care of it," Forest said firmly. "I'll take care of her."

"Just let me out of here." Patience's cranky voice filled the air. "I'm fine and I'm not staying here for another minute."

Sawyer shot a quick look at Forest. "If you're planning on being with her for the next couple of days, even though you're a big guy, I just hope the dragon lady doesn't eat you alive."

Chapter 5

Dillon awaited them at the door to Patience's room. There was no way Patience wanted to deal with him or any questions he might have for her. She had a killer headache and was confused as hell. All she wanted to do was crawl into her bed and sleep forever.

"Ben called me," Dillon said as they approached the room. "Dusty told him that something had happened to Dr. Forbes and that I should have a talk with you."

He looked expectantly at Patience. She stared back at him, not knowing what to say. Forest had taken her room key from her in the car and he used it to open the door.

With a sigh of relief and without speaking, she went inside, leaving the two men in the darkness just outside her room door. She stumbled into the bathroom, certain that her head might explode at any moment. She took off her clothes, pulled her nightgown over her head and then got into bed and closed her eyes.

"...attacked and hit over the head."

"...see anything?"

"...she doesn't remember anything."

Snatches of conversation drifted in from her open door. Shut up, she wanted to scream. She wanted the door closed and no noise at all, but her head hurt too badly to get out of bed and accomplish what she wanted.

Even though she wanted to quiet her brain, the confusion inside refused to be silent. What had happened to her? The last thing she remembered was placing the final bone in skeleton three. Everything that had occurred after that was shrouded in darkness until she'd regained consciousness in the car in front of the hospital.

Tears welled up as her head continued to bang with a force she'd never experienced before. She sucked them back, grateful that the only light in the room was that which flowed from the tiny bathroom.

She hoped that when Dillon and Forest finished their conversation, one of them would close her door so she could just quiet her mind and go to sleep. She'd be fine in the morning if she could just get some blessed sleep and rid herself of her torturous headache.

The voices outside her door stopped and a few minutes later her door closed, but she knew she wasn't alone. "Forest?" she guessed without opening her eyes. She could tell it was him by his scent, a clean smell of the outdoors with a hint of fresh fragrant cologne.

"Yeah, I'm right here in the chair."

She cracked open an eyelid and peered across the small room. He sat in the straight-backed chair against the wall, wearing his holster and gun and holding what appeared to be a small flashlight. "What are you doing in here?" She closed her eye once again.

"I'm going to be here with you all night. It's what the doctor ordered."

She wanted to protest. Doctor or no doctor, she didn't want or need Forest sitting with her all night. She wanted to rant and rail, but her headache made it impossible.

"I don't like this," she finally managed to say. "I don't like it at all."

"It doesn't matter whether you like it or not. For the next couple of days you aren't in charge of you," he replied easily.

"If I didn't have a headache that's about to kill me, I'd force you to leave this room right now. I'd scream and curse and drive you away with all of my viciousness."

He released a small, deep laugh. "You and what army?"

She cracked open one eye again and gave him the most baleful look she could muster before a groan escaped her.

"Would a cool cloth on your forehead help?" he asked sympathetically.

She didn't want anything from him. She didn't want him to be in the privacy of her room, but the thought of a cool washcloth across her banging forehead sounded like Heaven. "Please," she said, hating the faint whimper in her voice.

The chair creaked slightly, indicating that he'd gotten up. The sound of water running in the sink made her want to weep in anticipation of something...anything that might ease the grip of her headache. The water stopped running and then the cool cloth touched her forehead.

For a rough, tough cowboy, he had a gentle touch. He moved the folded cloth softly until it was perfectly centered on her forehead and then returned to the chair that squeaked as he sat back down. She had no memory of anyone ever touching her so tenderly, of anyone attempting to soothe her in any way.

"Better?" he asked after a few minutes had passed.

"A little. Why are you here with me?"

"You have a concussion. You shouldn't be left alone."

"Why can't I remember what happened to me?"

"Because you have a concussion. Patience, try not to worry. Don't overthink things. Just relax and rest. That's what the doctor said you need more than anything right now. Don't work your brain at all."

"I'll be fine in the morning," she said more to herself than to him. She had to be fine. She had work to do and people depending on her. Already too much time had passed on this particular job.

"You'll be in that bed for at least tomorrow," he countered. "Doctor's orders and we never argue with the doctor."

She said nothing. She didn't have the wherewithal to argue with him or anyone else tonight, but she couldn't just laze around in bed for a whole day. That's not what she did. But she'd worry about fighting him in the morning when she felt better.

She must have fallen asleep, for the next thing she knew he was calling her name. "I need to check your pupils," he said.

"Okay," she replied. The brightness of his flashlight shone first in one eye and then in the other.

"Looks good," he said and the light disappeared and he returned to his chair.

"Are you going to stay awake all night to do that?" she asked.

"That's the plan," he replied. "Don't worry about me, I've stayed up many nights before. I've ridden in the cattle herd through nights when we believed predators were near or when a cow was about to give birth. Taking care of you for the night is my pleasure."

Patience closed her eyes once again and fought against the sting of tears. Jeez, the concussion must be making her unusually emotional.

At no time in her life, at no time during her childhood had somebody taken care of her...especially not with pleasure. When her mother had been in the house, life had been all about her drama, with little attention paid to her daughter.

When her mother had left, her father certainly hadn't been a warm and fuzzy caretaker. She couldn't remember a single kiss, a stroke across the brow or a gentle pat on the shoulder.

Although tenderness and nurturing wasn't in her DNA, she couldn't help but be grateful that Forest was with her tonight and it apparently was in his genes.

"Tell me more about your childhood, about when your parents were alive," she said, knowing that falling back asleep would take a little time. At least her headache had eased somewhat, which was a blessing.

"My parents were the greatest," he began. "From the time I was old enough to notice, their love for one another was palpable. Dad was a charmer and a tease and Mom laughed at all of his bad jokes. She allowed him to be himself and loved him for it."

"What did they do for a living?" she asked.

"Dad was an insurance salesman and Mom was a second-grade school teacher. We ate dinner together every night and had family Friday nights when we ate popcorn and watched movies together." There was a soft wistfulness in his voice.

The chair squeaked, indicating that he'd shifted positions. "The day they died I thought my life was over. When I took to the streets I didn't much care what happened to me. I felt like a dead man walking."

"And then you came here and that changed," she murmured. His voice was so deep, so hypnotically smooth she was growing drowsier by the moment.

"Cass Holiday definitely changed my life. She embraced me like a son, she taught me how to find joy in working hard and bonding with the other young men who worked the ranch. She gave me back a family, different than the one I'd had, but family nevertheless."

She was awakened once again for her pupils to be checked. And so the night passed with her dozing between checks until the light of dawn drifted through her small window.

When she woke up to the early new day she looked over at Forest, who was asleep in the chair. He sat straight up, his head leaning slightly backward against the wall. His strong jaw held a shadow of dark whiskers and his mouth was slightly open, although no snores came from within.

He was definitely a handsome man and physically he stirred something deep inside her, but it frightened her—the pull she felt toward him. She didn't want to be pulled toward anyone. She'd always been alone and that was the way she liked it, the way it was supposed to be.

She closed her eyes once again. One thing was certain, despite her bravado and positive attitude the night before, she knew she couldn't work today. A bone-weary exhaustion gripped her, partially from being awakened so often during the night and also from the trauma she had suffered. Her brain still felt slightly scrambled.

What had happened to her? Would she ever remember? Since everyone assumed she had been attacked, then by who and why? She knew that when she and Devon had ventured into town and to the café for dinner a few nights before there had been a couple of men she hadn't been particularly friendly with. But if this had been their retribution for unfriendliness then she'd hate to see what they might do to somebody who really ticked them off.

She must have fallen asleep again, for the scent of bacon roused her back to consciousness. She opened her eyes to see Forest holding a bed tray with a plate of food and a built-in cup holder that carried a glass of orange juice.

Once again he was stepping all over her personal boundaries, but it was hard to be too mad at him when the scent of bacon filled the air.

"I'd be really upset about this if I wasn't so weak," she said and sat up against the bed pillows so that he could place the tray over her waist. It was strange that she was in bed, in her nightgown, and yet felt no self-consciousness about his presence.

"How's your head this morning?" he asked, obviously ignoring her touch of crankiness.

"The headache is gone. I just feel so weak and I'm still so confused about what happened to me."

"Don't think, just eat." He sat in the chair where he'd spent the night. He'd apparently taken the time while she'd snoozed to have a quick shower and shave. The morning whiskers she'd spied earlier were gone; he smelled of fresh-scented soap and wore clean jeans and a white T-shirt that stretched over his broad shoulders.

"I'm used to taking care of myself," she said as she picked up the fork.

"Everybody needs somebody at times in their lives. For you this is one of those times," he replied. "You just need to deal with it."

"This is the first time in my entire life and hopefully it will be the last." She took a bite of scrambled eggs and realized that as good as it smelled, she didn't have much of an appetite.

"There's nothing wrong with needing other people in your life," he countered.

She set her fork down and picked up a piece of bacon. Bacon she could always do. "And who do you need?"

"It depends. When I need a little music, I go to Mac McBride, who plays the guitar and sings like an angel. When I want a good laugh I usually go to Dusty. When I need somebody to set me straight, I talk to Brody Booth, who is a bit of a hard-ass and always tells me what he thinks. Different people serve different needs."

He leaned back in the chair and his gaze grew softer as he stared at some distance over her head. "Someday I hope to have a woman in my life that I want, that I need to stand by my side, to give me children and to love me until the end of time. I want that…I need that in my life."

Patience fought the impulse to scoff at him. Just because she didn't believe that kind of a relationship was possible didn't mean anything she said would change his mind about such nonsense.

She finished two pieces of bacon, drank the orange juice and then told him she was finished. He frowned, but took the tray from her lap. "I'm going to return this to the dining room, but you have to promise me that you won't move an inch from that bed while I'm gone."

"I promise," she replied. It was an easy promise to make because she didn't feel like moving. She didn't want to think or feel. She just wanted to be left alone until she could get back to work. But she knew she couldn't work today.

Tomorrow. She'd rest for today and then she'd be back at work tomorrow. Dillon was depending on her to complete the job. Cassie was eager to get the crime scene cleaned up. Patience's own reputation was at risk if she languished in bed for longer than a day.

She huddled back beneath the sheet and closed her eyes. She sensed Forest returning to her room. Did he intend to just sit in the chair and stare at her all day long? Surely he had better things to do.

"Patience, Dillon is here to speak to you," Forest said with a hint of reluctance. Instantly her headache returned. He was going to make her think. He was going to ask her questions to which she had no answers.

Yet she wanted answers, too. She needed to know who had attacked her in the darkness of the night. She sighed wearily and nodded to Forest, fighting against a faint shiver that threatened to walk up her spine.

Who had attacked her and why?

The last thing Forest wanted was for Patience to be stressed, and it was definitely stress lines that danced across her forehead when Dillon stepped into the small room.

She sat up, her face far too pale, and her hand shook slightly as she reached up and tucked an errant curl behind her ear.

"I don't think this is such a great idea," Forest said. "Maybe you should talk to her tomorrow. Clayton said her brain shouldn't be strained. Besides, she doesn't remember what happened to her last night." He looked at Patience for confirmation.

"The only thing I remember from last night is working in the tent," she said to Dillon. "I don't remember anything that happened after that."

"The questions I have for her don't pertain to last

night and I promise I'll be as brief as possible," Dillon said.

"It's okay," Patience replied and gestured Dillon into the chair where Forest had spent the long night.

Forest remained just inside the room. There was no way Dillon was going to exhaust or make Patience anxious, not on his watch.

Dillon pulled out a pad and pen. "I need to know if you've made any enemies while you've been here. Is there anyone you can think of who might want to do you harm?"

Patience's small burst of laughter surprised Forest. "If I was to guess, Chief Bowie, you'd be right up there at the top of the list," she replied.

Dillon's cheeks flushed faintly. "I'll admit we initially butted heads."

"I was just protecting the burial site," she replied.

"Okay, so take me off your list and tell me who else you might have made angry," Dillon said.

"Probably everyone on this ranch," she said. "I haven't exactly been the face of friendliness while I've been here."

"None of the men here would ever hurt Patience, no matter how cranky she's been," Forest exclaimed. "I mean, not that she's been really cranky with anyone in particular," he added in an effort not to offend.

"I've been a rip-roaring witch to almost everyone who has gotten in my path," she said and then frowned. "I did have a little run-in with a couple of men at the café when I went there for dinner with Devon the other night."

"What were their names?" Forest asked. He'd love to find the person or persons responsible for Patience's condition and crack a jaw or two.

"I have no idea. They were rude and vulgar and I told them so. Devon would know their names. I think he eats with them on a regular basis." She leaned her head back against the pillow, exhaustion once again playing across her features.

"I think that's enough questioning for now," Forest said as protectiveness surged up inside him. "Maybe we should go have a talk with Devon."

He knew it wasn't his place to intrude into Dillon's investigation, but he wanted to hear the names of those men, one of whom might have attacked Patience.

Dillon got up from the chair and Forest looked at Patience. "If you remember anything else, call me," Dillon said.

She nodded, closed her eyes and then waved a hand to dismiss both men. Forest pulled her door closed and then he and Dillon headed toward the huge white recreational vehicle parked near the blue tent that sheltered the burial site.

When they came to the area where Forest had found Patience unconscious on the ground the night before, his heart beat a bit faster.

If the blow to her head had been a little harder, if it had landed just an inch or so to the right, then she might have been found dead instead of just suffering from a concussion.

His hands clenched into fists at his sides. Anger was

normally an alien emotion to Forest, but the attack on Patience had awakened a rage-filled beast inside him.

"While you were at the hospital last night, several of my men and I swept the area looking for something, anything that might provide a clue," Dillon said.

"And I'm assuming you found nothing. Otherwise you would have already mentioned it to me by now."

"You're right," Dillon replied in obvious frustration. "We didn't find whatever she was hit with or any sign that anyone was on the property who didn't belong."

He cast a sideways glance at Forest. "I know all of you men here share a special bond with each other, but that doesn't mean there might not be a bad apple in the bunch."

Forest shook his head. "You'll have to prove that to me before I'll ever believe it," he said firmly. The men on this ranch had all grown up together.

They weren't just a dozen cowboys working on the same ranch. They were brothers, hardened by loss and dysfunction at an early age and then made whole again by Cass Holiday's firm but loving hands and bonded together like family.

Forest had worked with, laughed and confided to his "brothers" for almost sixteen years. Together they had mourned deeply Cass's death almost three months earlier in a tornado. It would take one hell of a lot of cold, hard evidence for him to believe any of the men here had a rotten core.

Dillon knocked on the trailer's door and it took only a moment for Devon to answer. "Chief... Forest," he said and stepped down the stairs, closing the door to the trailer behind him. "How's Dr. Forbes doing?" he asked Forest. "Sawyer told me last night she'd refused to stay at the hospital and that you were looking after her."

"She'll be all right, but she won't be working for the next day or two," Forest replied.

"But that doesn't mean you can't continue the work," Dillon said.

Devon looked utterly horrified, his brown eyes behind his glasses widening. "Are you kidding me? She would kill me if I touched anything in that tent without her being present." He shook his head. "If she's not working for a couple of days, then neither am I. That's the way it goes."

"I have a couple of questions to ask you," Dillon said.

Devon frowned. "If it's about whatever happened here last night then I can't help you. I heard a commotion and came out of the trailer, but that was after whatever happened to Dr. Forbes."

"No, it's about the times you and Dr. Forbes went into town to the café for dinner," Dillon said.

Devon's frown deepened. "What about them?"

"Patience told us she had a little unpleasant encounter with a couple of men at the café," Forest said. "She thought you would know their names."

"It really wasn't a big deal," Devon said. "A couple of the men got a little mouthy with her and she retaliated. I'm sure you're both aware that Dr. Forbes can have a very sharp tongue at times."

"I'd like more detail about what happened and the names of those men," Forest said firmly.

Devon shrugged. "They'd heard Dr. Forbes had been

referred to as the dragon lady around here and they wanted to know if she was as hot in the sack as she was with her temper."

"Names," Forest said as his anger rose up again inside him.

"Zeke Osmond and Shep Harmon. I think Greg Albertson might have been there, too," Devon said after a moment of hesitation.

"I should have known," Forest said in disgust. Humes ranch hands. He knew none of the Holiday men would ever talk to a woman that way. Forest narrowed his eyes and looked over toward the property line that divided the Holiday land from the Humes place.

"They've all been nice to me. I can't imagine any of them hurting Dr. Forbes because they all got a little mouthy with each other," Devon said defensively.

"You obviously don't know the true nature of the company you're keeping," Forest replied and looked back at the man.

Devon raised his square jaw. "Like I said, they've all been nice to me." He looked at Dillon. "Was there anything else you needed to know?"

"No, that should do it for now," Dillon replied.

Devon nodded and returned to the interior of the trailer.

Forest released a sigh of frustration. "You'd better check out where those men were and with whom last night when Patience was attacked. Otherwise I'll be more than happy to go over there right now and get some answers."

"Forest, we both know that's not a good idea. I'll

head to the Humes ranch now," Dillon said. "But you know at the moment we have nothing to implicate any of those men in any wrongdoing. I don't want you going off half-cocked and on a mission of retribution."

"I'll let you do your job," Forest replied evenly. "But there's something I'm sure you've already considered in this whole mess."

"And what's that?" Dillon asked.

"That whoever killed those people in that grave is possibly still around here and the moving of the bones and the attack on Patience is their way of slowing down the investigation. For the past fifteen years or so the killer has felt safe."

"If the tornado hadn't ripped that shed apart, he would still feel safe," Dillon replied with a frown.

"But now the crime has been exposed and Patience is the key to help solve the mystery."

"Even if the killer murders Patience, there will be another forensic anthropologist brought out here to continue the work," Dillon countered.

"And that will take more time and there's no way of knowing if each person who comes here to work the crime scene won't face the same kind of danger."

"So you think the killer is going to try to attack Patience again?"

Forest dropped his hand to the butt of his gun in his holster. "I think a killer is desperate to keep this burial scene from being fully processed and that means Patience is definitely in danger. She doesn't know it yet, but she's just inherited a full-time bodyguard."

"She's probably not going to be happy about that," Dillon said ruefully.

"I'm not taking on the job of making her happy," Forest said with determination. "I'm taking on the job of keeping her alive."

Chapter 6

Patience slept most of the day away. She was grateful that, for the most part, Forest left her alone, only popping his head in the door a couple of times to see if she needed anything.

It was late afternoon when she finally crawled out of bed, feeling better than she had all day. She reached up and touched what had been a goose egg the night before and was now just a tender lump on the back of her head.

She needed to shower and get dressed. Even though she wouldn't be working or doing much of anything else, she just wanted to feel somewhat human again.

She peeled off her nightgown and threw it into a laundry bag on the floor of the small bathroom. She knew there was a washing machine and dryer that the cowboys used. She'd already washed clothes there several times since her arrival at the ranch. Maybe she'd spend what was left of the late afternoon doing a load of laundry. That shouldn't strain her brain too much.

The shower was heavenly. The warm spray drizzled her from head to toe. Thankfully, other than the tenderness on her scalp, the headache was completely gone and she had no other aches or pains.

It was strange. Somebody had attacked her and she knew she should be afraid, but having no memory of the actual attack made it difficult for her to work up any genuine fear for her safety, other than an occasional faint shiver up her spine when she focused on the idea of being attacked.

If the person who had hit her over the head had really wanted to hurt her, he would have used a meat cleaver and split her head wide open, the way someone had killed the young men she'd found in the ground.

If the attacker had wanted her dead, he could have stabbed her in the back rather than clobber her over the head. Apparently he hadn't wanted another murder investigation taking place on the property.

She gently shampooed her hair and tried to empty her mind of all thoughts. She hated to admit it, but Forest was right; thinking too hard threatened to bring back the headache that she was so grateful was now gone.

Laundry was all she needed to take care of today and by tomorrow she'd be ready to face the bones again. She finished the shower and dressed in a pair of navy capris and a red and white button-up sleeveless blouse.

She grabbed her laundry bag from the bathroom,

a plastic bag of detergent pods and then opened the room door.

"What do you think you're doing?" Forest sat in a chair just outside of his room.

"Laundry. Or am I now some kind of a prisoner?" she asked.

He rose from his chair and gestured for her to hand him the cotton bag of dirty clothing. "I just don't want to see you doing too much. You're still in recovery mode."

She tightened her grip on the bag. "I think I can manage throwing some clothes into a machine and turning it on. I'm feeling much better." Her hold on the bag was now a death grip. "Trust me, I've got this."

"Okay, then I'll just walk with you to the laundry room."

She wanted to be cross with him, to tell him that she didn't need him or his presence. But her mind filled with the thought of him sitting in a hard-backed chair throughout the night, of the soft slide of a cool cloth across her forehead, and it was impossible to be irritated with him.

"Suit yourself," she finally replied and headed to the opposite end of the cowboy motel where the laundry room was located.

"I think it would be a good idea for you to join us for dinner in the cowboy dining room tonight," he said as she began to load the washing machine.

She stopped what she was doing and turned to look at him. "Why would I want to do that?"

"You barely touched the breakfast I brought to you and you refused lunch. You need a good hot meal, and the dining room is the best option for that." His blue eyes held more than a hint of determination that she didn't have the energy to protest.

It was just one meal, she told herself. "Fine," she said and turned back to finish loading the clothes. She tossed in a detergent pod, started the machine and then turned to face him once again.

He smiled, that ridiculous gesture crinkling his eyes with warmth and stirring an equally ridiculous response of heat in her. "I'm glad you agreed," he said over the sound of the washing machine filling with water. "I was afraid I'd have to carry you over my shoulder and tie you to a bench in the dining room."

"How long do you intend to run my life?" She crossed her arms as if that might keep her safe from the flitter of heat his smile had evoked.

"At least for the next day or so. After that we'll see how stubborn you are."

"I'm planning on getting back to work tomorrow."

"That's not happening," he replied, again with a touch of surprising stubbornness in his voice. "The doctor said you need a couple of days of brain rest. I've already got a nice day of relaxation planned for you for tomorrow."

She shoved past him and out of the laundry room. He followed closely at her heels as she walked back to her room. A day of relaxation…she didn't even know what that might look like. She didn't do relaxation. She worked.

When she reached her room she turned to look at him once again. "I can't just stay away from the tent forever, Forest. I have people depending on me to get the job done."

"I understand that, but you are also recuperating from a head injury and one more day isn't going to make that much difference in the investigation." He looked at his watch. "By the time your laundry is finished it will be time for us to head to the dining room."

"I don't like this," she exclaimed. She'd always maintained tight control of every aspect in her life, and at the moment everything had spiraled completely out of her control. It was a scary feeling that threatened to close up the back of her throat and made her want to wail in protest.

"I didn't figure you would, but I'm only looking after your well-being." A softness flowed from his gaze, a softness that was both earnest and caring.

She needed to get away from him. A lump had leapt to her throat and her eyes burned with the unfamiliar sensation of impending tears. What was wrong with her? What was it about this man that made her want to shed tears?

"I'll see you at dinnertime," she said and made a quick entrance into her room.

She sat on the edge of her bed, her brain still filled with his words, the truth that had flowed from his gaze. Nobody had ever cared much about her well-being. Certainly not her mother before she'd left the marriage and then her child, and definitely not her father who had been a cold and unemotional man when he was present at all.

Why did this gentle giant of a cowboy care about

her when nobody else ever had? Even Devon hadn't come to check on her since she'd been hit in the head, although she was sure he was probably getting updates from somebody.

What had she done to earn Forest's concern for her? What had she done to gain what appeared to be a genuine softness for her in him?

When she left her room a half an hour later to move her laundry from the washer to the dryer, Forest was at the side of the building pulling weeds. When her clothes were dry he was back in the chair just outside his door.

"Ready for dinner?" he asked and rose as she opened her door to place her clean clothes inside. He stood in her doorway as she set the neatly folded items on the bed.

"You know I don't like this," she repeated to him.

He grinned. "You don't like a lot of things, but it will be good for you to step out of your comfort zone for a little while."

She sighed, locked her door and pulled it closed behind her, and then together they headed around the building to the back, where the cowboy dining room was located.

She was like a cow going to slaughter, nervous about a different experience and unsure of what to expect. Did cows even have feelings…fears? Good grief, her brain was definitely still scrambled if she was thinking about how cattle felt.

"Don't be nervous," Forest said as if he read her mind and to her surprise he grabbed her hand with his. Big and strong, his slightly calloused hand swallowed hers in a pleasant, reassuring warmth. "I'm fairly certain that no one among the men there is a human-eating zombie."

A burst of laughter bubbled out of her. "I can honestly say that thought never entered my mind."

"Trust me, you will be treated not only with respect by all of the men, but also to a terrific meal provided by Cookie," he replied.

"I haven't earned any respect or goodwill from anyone while I've been here," she said with a touch of chagrin. Forest's kindness had shone an uncomfortable light on her own behavior since she'd been on the ranch.

He squeezed her hand. "Just relax and enjoy this new experience. Don't think about anything else."

As they entered the dining room Patience's first impression was of controlled chaos. Long picnic tables were set up in the center of the huge room and nine cowboys were seated there, silverware clinking and laughter ringing as they enjoyed their evening meal together.

It was obvious the room was not just a dining area, but also a hangout as one section held several sofas and easy chairs and a television.

It was the buffet table that captured her attention as hunger pangs shot through her stomach. She was suddenly starving. Thick slices of ham were on a tray next to a huge bowl of fried potatoes and onions. Bright red sliced tomatoes competed in color with a pan of steamed yellow and orange squash. A basket held yeasty dinner rolls the size of her palm.

Forest handed her a plate and she began to fill it, as he moved just behind her, heaping food on his own plate. "Forest… Dr. Forbes, over here."

The blond cowboy she recognized as Dusty waved them to empty spots at his picnic table. She followed Forest and they slid onto the bench seat side by side with Dusty across the table from them.

"I'll go grab our silverware and drinks," Forest said. "Iced tea okay?"

"Fine," she replied, nerves immediately jangling inside her as he got up and left her at the table.

"Dr. Forbes, how are you feeling?" Dusty asked.

"Much better, thank you, and please call me Patience."

"Okay," he replied, looking pleased. "Patience, I've got to tell you, you definitely scared the heck out of all of us," Dusty said. His blue eyes narrowed. "We don't like the idea of anyone hurting one of our own, especially a woman."

"I can hardly be considered one of your own," she protested. "I'm just here to do a job."

"As long as you're on this property, you're one of us," Dusty exclaimed firmly.

One of us…the words held such a surprising, welcoming ring. She'd never been one of anything before. She'd always been just one.

Forest returned to the table and while they ate he and Dusty filled her in on who was who among the ranch hands. "The cowboy with the blond hair over there is Clay Madison. He's our resident womanizer, and the man next to him is Tony Nakni. Tony is Choctaw Indian." Dusty flashed his dimples in a grin. "I keep trying to get him to teach me some of the Choctaw dances and traditions, but he tells me when I dance I look like a rubber chicken on steroids."

Patience grinned and realized why Forest had remained so close to Dusty. He seemed refreshingly open and honest. As the meal continued, she learned the names of the other men... Brody Booth, Mac McBride, Sawyer Quincy, Flint McCay, Jerod Steen and foreman Adam Benson.

When she left the dining room she'd probably be unable to name most of them, but there was no question that there was a strong bond among the men. They teased each other unmercifully and laughed both at themselves and at each other. There was warmth in the room, the warmth of caring and men who looked after each other.

It was definitely an unfamiliar atmosphere for Patience and as she listened to the laughter and talk whirling around her, she did relax and enjoy the delicious meal.

The only person who didn't interact with the others was Cookie, who stood at the end of the buffet table like an island unto himself. He was a daunting figure with his muscular build, buzz-cut black hair and dark eyes.

After the meal was finished, Forest talked her into staying for a little while to listen to Mac McBride play his guitar. Several of the cowboys, including Mac, moved to the sofas, and Patience recognized that this was probably something that happened on a regular basis.

By the time Mac had strummed a couple of chords, she recognized that he wasn't just a cowboy who occasionally tinkered at playing. He was a talented musician who not only played well, but as Forest had mentioned, also had the deep, soothing voice of an angel.

After the fourth song, Patience touched Forest's forearm to tell him she was ready to leave. He took one look at her features and stood.

"You could have stayed," she said as he walked her out of the dining room. "As much as I was enjoying myself, I'm exhausted."

"I was ready to go anyway," he replied.

They were quiet until they reached her room. "Surely you aren't planning on checking my pupils all night again tonight," she said as she pulled her room key out of her pocket.

"I don't think that's necessary. But I would prefer you not leave your room alone either tonight or tomorrow."

She looked up at him, his eyes taking on the faint violet hue of the twilight that surrounded them. "You think I'm in danger." It was a statement, not a question.

He hesitated a moment and then nodded somberly. "Even though you don't remember it, you were viciously attacked. Until we know why or by whom, I don't want you alone anywhere. It might have been the result of the unpleasant conversation you had with some of the Humes ranch hands at the café. I haven't heard anything from Dillon today, but I don't want you in a vulnerable position all alone again."

"Does that mean I've just gained a bodyguard?" she asked.

He smiled. "Yeah, and I already know you don't like it, but until somebody is in jail for attacking you or you finish up your work and leave here, you have your own personal bodyguard."

"But you have your own work to do here at the ranch," she protested.

"During the days when you're in the tent doing your thing, I'll be in the corral working with the horse. When you're safe in your room, I'll be in mine. If you decide to go anywhere for any reason, you need to make sure I'm with you." His gaze was once again somber. "This isn't optional, Patience."

She hesitated a moment and then nodded. "Okay. Good night, Forest." She unlocked her door and opened it.

"Tomorrow you stay in your room until I come and get you. I've got the day planned out for us, and then the next day if you feel like it you can get back to your bones."

Once again she nodded and then with a wave of her hand she stepped into her room and closed and locked the door behind her. She tried not to think as she undressed, pulled on her nightgown, turned out the light and then curled up in the bed.

It was really too early to go to sleep, but she was tired and didn't even feel like reading one of her tabloids. Instead, in the darkness of the room, her mind began to whirl.

She'd hated the very idea of eating in the cowboy dining room and yet had found the experience quite pleasant. All of the men had been kind to her, each of them at one time or another inquiring how she felt, did she need more tea, was she ready for dessert?

Her thoughts shifted to her final conversation with Forest and the fear that had been missing from her since the attack appeared like a quivering ball of anxiety in the pit of her stomach.

Forest believed she was in danger, and it was impossible for her to find facts to cling to in order to prove otherwise. Had the blow to her head been the result of her verbal altercation with the creepy men in the café? Or had it been something far more ominous?

Was the person who had killed the young men in the pit determined to keep the rest of the bones from being processed? Was she perceived as the greatest risk of uncovering the secret of the killer's identity?

Had the whack over her head been a simple assault or attempted murder? A chill danced up her spine as her mouth dried.

Was it possible she'd just dined with a man who wanted her dead? Forest had designated himself to be her bodyguard, but like the other cowboys he'd been at the ranch when the murders had occurred.

She wanted to trust him. She needed to trust him, but she couldn't help a little bit of doubt that darkened her heart.

It was just after ten the next morning when Forest knocked on Patience's door. He had everything prepared for what he hoped would be a relaxing, non-stressful day for the two of them. The Wednesday morning sun was brilliant, but a slight breeze promised a day not quite as hot as the days that had passed since July had swept in.

The weather report had indicated a possible rain storm late that evening. All the ranchers in the area would appreciate the rain. It had been far too long since they'd had any precipitation to ease the summer drought.

Patience opened her door and Forest's appreciation for potential rain shifted to a burst of pleasure at the sight of her. She wasn't dressed in anything special, just denim capris and a lavender sleeveless button-up blouse that enhanced the red of her hair and the bright green of her eyes.

"You know I feel well enough to get back to work," she said in greeting.

"And we agreed that you'd take today off and we'll see how you feel tomorrow," he replied. "Besides, I've got the day all planned out and it doesn't require you using your brain power at all." Her eyes held a hint of distrust he hadn't seen there before. He frowned at her. "What are you thinking, Dr. Forbes?"

"Nothing," she replied. "I'm on notice not to think today." She stepped out of her room and closed the door behind her. "So, what are we doing?"

"The first thing on the agenda is stopping by the dining room to get a duffel that Cookie has prepared." They walked side by side and Forest continued talking. "I spent all day yesterday trying to decide how I wanted you to relax today. I thought about taking you into town to have lunch at Tammy's Tea House."

"Tammy's Tea House—that doesn't sound like a place where a cowboy would be comfortable," she replied.

"Especially a big cowboy trying to maneuver dainty

little tea cups and sandwiches the size of my thumb." He flashed her a quick smile. "Besides, you don't strike me as the kind of woman who would be impressed in a place that has pink tablecloths and girly decorations."

"And what kind of a woman do I strike you as?" she asked in obvious curiosity.

Forest stopped walking and gazed at her thoughtfully. "I'm not quite sure yet. I'm still trying to figure you out."

By that time they had reached the dining room entrance. The room was empty, as it was too late for breakfast and too early for lunch.

Cookie appeared from the kitchen with a duffel bag that also had a cooler area inside. "That should be everything you need," he said as he handed it to Forest.

"Thanks, Cookie, I appreciate it."

Cookie gave a curt nod and then disappeared back into the kitchen.

"What's in the bag?" Patience asked.

"It's a secret," Forest replied with a mysterious smile as he and Patience stepped back outside into the bright sunshine.

"I just hope the contents don't contain a meat cleaver and a collapsible shovel," she replied.

Forest stopped in his tracks, appalled that the thought would even dare to enter her head. She stared downward, and he used his thumb and forefinger and took her chin to force her to look up at him.

"Patience, do you believe I killed those people?" He waved a hand in the direction of the blue tent, not looking away from her. "Do you really believe that I

attacked you and I'm just waiting for the perfect opportunity to kill you?" His voice held his own incredulity.

Her cheeks flushed with a pink hue. "All I know is
that at some point a long time ago six young men were
viciously murdered and at the time of the crime all of
you were working here at the ranch."

He dropped his hand from her chin, but their gazes
remained locked. In her eyes was a hint of doubt that
cut through to his heart. "Patience, all I can tell you
is that I'm a protective kind of man, not a killer, but
I know those are just words. I guess you're going to
have to get to know me better before you have whatever proof you need to completely trust me. Besides,
if I wanted to hurt or kill you, I could have done it the
night of the barn dance when nobody else was around.
I could have stepped on your throat the night I found
you unconscious in the grass. I've had a dozen oppor-
tunities where I could attack you and nobody would
be the wiser."

He gestured her toward the stables, a knot in his
stomach as he realized that she didn't trust him. And
yet he asked himself, why should she trust anyone? Even
Dillon had intimated that the killer could be right here
working on the property.

She must trust him more than she thought she did,
he consoled himself as they entered the darker interior of the stable. After all, she had no idea what he
had planned for her today and yet here she was right
by his side. He had his gun in its holster on his belt.
She was going to some unknown place with an armed
man. Didn't that imply a modicum of faith on her part?

"I'm pretty sure cleaning out horse stalls isn't considered relaxing," she said as they walked deeper into the building that smelled not just of fresh hay and leather but also of animal musk.

"On the contrary, it can be very relaxing," he protested. "Especially with a collapsible shovel," he added teasingly. "Actually, the bag is packed with a picnic lunch and I thought it would be nice if we took a horseback ride out on the property and I could show you something besides the interior of that blue tent."

"I don't know how to ride," she said. "I've never been on a horse before." Nerves deepened her voice.

"I wouldn't let you ride on your own," he replied. "I already checked with Clayton to make sure you could get on a horse and he said it was fine as long as it's for a slow, easy ride. You'll be with me on my horse and that way I can assure a comfortable and safe ride for you."

They reached the stall where Thunder was housed. Patience looked at the large horse and then at Forest. "Let me guess, his name is Demon or Devil."

Forest laughed. "Actually, her name is Thunder and she's a great horse. You'll be fine on her with me. Why don't you have a seat over on that bale of hay while I saddle her up."

"Are you sure this is a good idea?" she asked.

"I think it's a great idea." He led Thunder from the stall and quickly set to gearing up one of his favorite companions for a day of leisure.

"Was she a wild horse you worked with?" Patience asked.

"No, Cass bought her for me because she was big

and strong. I trained her and she's been mine since she was old enough to ride. She has a gentle soul and is always eager to please."

"If she's that nice then she'll probably buck me right off for being the dragon lady," Patience replied.

"Thunder would never do anything so unlady-like," he replied. "Besides, you haven't turned into a dragon in days."

It took him only minutes to saddle up the horse and fasten both the duffel and a rolled-up clean, soft blanket to the back of the saddle, then he turned and looked at Patience. "Ready?"

"Probably not," she replied, although she stood and walked closer. "What do I have to do?"

"Nothing except straddle the saddle." Before she could protest or have any more time to think, he grabbed her by the waist and lifted her up and into the saddle.

She was light as a feather and he would have much rather pulled her against his chest in a tight embrace than seat her on the horse. But today wasn't about his wants or needs. It was about her and keeping her body and brain as relaxed as possible.

She gasped in surprise and clutched the saddle horn in a death grip. "What happens now?"

"I'm going to get into the saddle behind you," he said. "Don't be afraid and stay just where you are in the seat."

He wasn't worried about them being squished together. His saddle was large and she was small. They would easily be able to ride double.

He stepped into the stirrup and swung his leg up and

over to the other side. As he settled in just behind her the scent of her hair filled his head. Peaches. Fresh, ripe peaches, he'd never noticed it before and now fought the impulse to lean forward and bury his face in the sweet scent and red silky curls.

He reached around her for the reins and caught a whiff of the floral fragrance of her light perfume. With a flick of the reins Thunder walked out of the stable and into the sunshine.

When they started toward the distant pasture, Patience held herself stiff and tall in the saddle. "You need to relax," he said. "Let your body relax and your hips roll with the horse's gait. It will give you a much better, more comfortable ride."

She nodded and the tension slowly left her body. As she relaxed her butt slid against him and the contact, combined with the heady scent of her, stirred a fiery flame inside him.

He hadn't considered how her intimate nearness would affect him and now that was all he could think about. The breeze lifted her hair from the nape of her neck and he knew the skin there would be soft and kissable.

He wanted to stop the horse, spread out the blanket and forget all about lunch. He'd rather kiss her until she couldn't think, slowly remove her clothes so he could caress every inch of her body. He wanted to make love to her until she believed in fairy tales and happily-ever-after, until she believed that science and facts weren't the answer to everything.

Unfortunately he wasn't going to do any of those

things. In any case she'd given him no indication that she was even open to a single kiss from him.

For her this was meant to be a day to continue her healing process. For him, it promised to be a long, torturous day of tamping down his desire for a woman who was all wrong for him.

Chapter 7

She was on a horse. It was nothing short of amazing. She had never thought about taking a horseback ride before, but she relaxed with each step that the horse took away from the blue tent and the tedious yet important work that still awaited her.

It didn't take long for her to be so relaxed that her back rested comfortably against Forest's broad chest. In the back of her mind a little voice whispered that she should straighten up a bit, remove the physical contact that was far more intimate than she'd shared with any man for a very long time.

Still, it wasn't just the gun in the holster around his waist that made her feel safe, it was the broadness, the very strength of his body against hers.

She was probably a fool for trusting him, knowing

that Dillon had all the ranch cowboys on his list as potential suspects of the long-ago murders. She apparently was all kinds of fool, for without any real evidence, she did trust Forest to be a good guy.

Besides, he'd been right. If he had really wanted to hurt or kill her, he could have accomplished it a dozen times when they'd been alone with no witnesses around.

It had been obvious the night before that Dusty worshipped Forest, probably due to that time on the streets when Forest had been Dusty's hero and had saved him from being preyed on by bigger, stronger boys. It had also been apparent that all of the other men held both respect and great affection for the big cowboy.

Forest had nursed her through a long night with the gentle caring of a mama bear tending to a wounded cub. He'd rushed her to the hospital when she'd been unconscious and completely vulnerable. She trusted the people she worked with because they had credentials to prove that they were professionals. To her surprise, she trusted Forest on a gut instinct she hadn't known she possessed.

Despite not having any real concrete evidence that he was the good guy she believed him to be, the warmth of his body, the press of his thighs against hers made her feel safe and protected and more than just a little bit hot and bothered.

She focused on the pastoral scenery that surrounded them, shoving away inappropriate thoughts of the man in the saddle behind her.

The Holiday Ranch was a vast operation, with plenty

of large and small outbuildings and pasture as far as the eye could see.

The air smelled of grass and cattle and sunshine and nothing like old bones or burial pits. She drew in a deep breath, giving herself permission to let her brain simply enjoy this novel experience, one she didn't expect would happen again.

Forest kept Thunder at an easy walk, and as they crested a hill, she caught her breath at the sight of hundreds of big black cattle. Riding among them were two men on horseback who waved at them as they moved down the rise.

"Are we going to picnic with cows?" she asked.

Forest laughed, his breath warm on the back of her neck. She fought against an unexpected shiver of sensual pleasure. "I promise you I haven't invited any cows to the lunch table. We're heading to a place on the property where the cows aren't allowed. There's a nice pond and great shade trees. It's near where Cookie lives in a small cabin."

They began to veer to the left, away from the herd of cattle and as they rode she asked questions about the various outbuildings they passed and what the cowboys they met were doing.

This was a view into a world she'd never encountered, far away from academia and crime scenes. Idyllic and peaceful, the landscape was definitely conducive to just being and not thinking.

She hated to admit it, but Forest had been right. She needed this extra day of no brain drain, of just enjoying the faint breeze on her face, of smelling the country air and the warmth and comfort of the man behind her.

Tomorrow would be time to get back to work, to dealing with the puzzle of the final skeletons and trying to discover anything that might help Dillon in his investigation to find out what had happened so long ago and who was responsible.

It took them almost an hour to reach the pond where the water sparkled in the sunshine and nearby ancient trees provided thick leafy shelter.

They dismounted and Forest loosely tied Thunder to a nearby tree, giving the horse plenty of leeway to amble about and snack on the sweet green grass beneath the tree.

He then spread a plaid blanket beneath one of the nearby trees. "Are you hungry?" he asked and unfastened the duffel bag.

She sat on the blanket and shook her head. "Not right now."

He joined her on the blanket and set the bag to the side. "I think this is one of the nicest places on the ranch." He pointed to the right where in the distance a small cabin could be seen. "That's Cookie's place. It used to belong to the ranch foreman, but when the foreman ran out on Cass and she hired Cookie, he took it over."

"What's his story? He doesn't seem to be much of a part of the rest of you other than feeding you."

Forest shrugged. "Nobody really knows his story. He's very private and was already working here when

I first arrived. I don't know who scared me more at that time, Cass or Cookie."

"Tell me more about Cass." She liked the sound of his deep voice and he had so much more life to talk about than she did. She stretched out on her side and propped her head up on one elbow.

His smile was soft and distant with obvious memories. "Cass was bigger than life. She could wield a bull-whip like a champion and was a stubborn and tough taskmaster. It was a gutsy thing to do, bringing in street kids she didn't know to work for her. But she was determined to transform this ranch, our lives and us and she managed to do it all. She wasn't just an employer. She became our mother, our mentor and made us into a family."

"You still miss her," Patience said.

"We all do," he agreed. "She gave us all a sense of self-worth and unconditional love we might have never found without her."

"What do you think about Cassie?" she asked of the new owner of the ranch.

"She's fine. She's come a long way since she first arrived in her fancy high heels and city clothes. She's worked closely with Adam to learn what she needs to know about running this place effectively. There is some doubt among the men as to just how committed she is to remaining here."

"Why?"

"We all know she still has a store in New York City. Some of us believe that she was going to sell the ranch, and then the skeletons were found." He stretched out to mirror her position on the blanket. "The crime scene definitely set back any plans she might have had to sell out. I guess time will tell what she decides to do. We can only hope that if she does sell the new owner will keep us all together on the ranch."

"It must be tough not being sure about your future," she replied. The sun shifted through the leaves and dappled his face in both light and shadows. Once again she was struck by his handsomeness.

"There was a time I didn't believe I had a future at all. Whatever happens now, we're all strong enough to roll with the punches. Did you always know what you wanted to do with your life?" he asked.

She frowned thoughtfully. "I'm not sure I ever made a conscious decision about it. It's what my father wanted me to do and so I did it. Thankfully it worked out because I love what I do."

"Me, too," he replied.

She moved her gaze to the right where beyond the pond six silos rose up from the ground. "What's in those?"

"They're filled with last year's corn. Eventually it will be sold to other ranchers to make room for this year's crop."

She looked back at him. "Silos have always scared me. I told Devon one time that they remind me of something otherworldly, something slightly ominous. I hate them."

His eyes twinkled. "And what facts do you base that feeling on, Dr. Forbes?"

Heat filled her cheeks and she contemplated whether

to tell him the truth or not. She finally opted for truth. "It was in the shadow of a silo that I lost my virginity to a callous college guy who had a bet with his frat brothers." She looked down at the blanket, shame washing over her as she thought of how stupid, how naive she'd been. "Afterward I was the laughingstock of the entire campus."

She didn't see his hand move, but suddenly it was on her cheek. She looked up into the simmering blue depths of his eyes. "You gave him a precious gift and he didn't take care of it."

His slightly calloused fingers moved tenderly on her skin, caressing her from the corner of her eye down to her trembling lips. "If I could, I'd take that memory away from you. If I could, I'd beat the hell out of that stupid frat boy."

She laughed and he dropped his hand back to the blanket. "I think I'm ready for lunch now." She didn't want to think about how much she'd liked his touch, how bereft she had felt when he'd withdrawn it.

She definitely didn't want to think of that traumatic event that had occurred next to a silo on a ranch just outside of Oklahoma City.

He sat up and grabbed the duffel and pulled it between them. "Let's see what goodies Cookie packed for us." He opened the bag and first withdrew two cold bottles of water, then began to lay out containers of a variety of food items.

"Fried chicken, potato salad, bread and butter sandwiches…it looks like Cookie intended us to stay out here for days," she exclaimed as he continued to pull food out of the duffel. There was also fresh fruit, slices of cheese and several thick, moist brownies.

"It wouldn't be a bad place to spend a couple of days," he replied when the bag was empty. "If you listen closely you can hear the splash of fish in the water and the birds singing in the trees."

She sat up and he handed her a paper plate, a napkin and a fork, and for the first time she noticed the musical birdsong, the ripple of water from the pond and from the distance the deep lowing of cattle.

"It is peaceful here," she said.

"Nature at its finest," he replied.

They fell silent as they filled their plates and began to eat. "You were right. I needed one more day and this is nice," she said after a few minutes.

"At least you haven't said you don't like it so far," Forest teased.

"I say that too much," she replied. "It means I'm uncomfortable with the situation."

"I'll keep that in mind for future purposes," he replied.

She took several bites and then eyed him curiously. "How can you just take off work to babysit me? I'm sure you have some sort of daily duties to attend to. Won't Cassie be upset with you?"

"It's not like I won't be doing any work at all. I still plan on working with the horse in the corral next to where you'll be working."

"But I know you have other duties expected of you besides that," she protested.

"Cassie knows how it is around here. If one of us

goes down for any reason, then the others pick up the slack. We all do everything on the ranch and pitch in to see that what needs to be done gets done each day. The others will cover for me until I'm working again."

"It's not like that on my job. Devon has the credentials that I have, but despite being older than me he doesn't have the same field experience." She wiped her fingers on her napkin and set her plate down next to her. "I'm totally stuffed."

"I'm getting there," he replied as he reached for another piece of chicken.

"Tell me more about your life with your parents," she said when they'd both finished eating.

She was once again stretched out on the blanket, him also on his side facing her. A pleasant drowsiness had swept over her. Her stomach was full, the shade was nice and the sounds of nature surrounded them.

"What do you want to know?" he asked.

"Anything…everything," she replied. She rolled over on her back and stared at the leaves above her. "Your family life was so different than mine. It's kind of like reading one of my tabloids. I find it interesting."

"Okay, then I'll start at the beginning. I weighed almost twelve pounds when I was born. My mother swore she felt like she was birthing a continent," he began.

She smiled. "Was your father a big man?"

"No, but apparently my grandfather was well over six feet tall and was considered a big guy. Anyway, from the time I was little my mother schooled me on the fact that I had to be extra careful not to hurt my friends because I was so much bigger than all of them."

"The gentle giant," she murmured.

"Something like that," he agreed. "My dad got me into football when I was six and I played in junior high. They attended every game, carrying silly signs to cheer me on. Every Sunday Mom made a pot roast and I'd wake up with the smell of it filling the house. We'd all sit down at noon for a big meal and then later that night we'd have leftovers while we watched television together."

That was the last thing she heard as she fell asleep and dreamed of a family life that included pot roast on Sundays and parents who cheered for their child's success.

Forest knew the precise moment she fell asleep: her chest rose and fell in slow, even rhythm and her eyes closed and remained closed even after he'd stopped speaking.

He watched her sleep, taking the advantage to admire the splay of her fiery hair against the blanket, the curve of her slightly parted lips and her petite but sexy body in complete repose.

Her eyelashes were long and her jawline sweetly curved to her strong, determined chin. He could look at her forever and find something new to admire…like the faint hint of freckles he'd never noticed before that danced across the bridge of her nose and across both shoulders.

He'd like to kiss each freckle. He'd like to give her a kiss that would awaken her like a sleeping princess.

But he was no prince. He was just an ill-educated cow-boy who had no business lusting after her.

Besides, he didn't care how long she slept. He wouldn't awaken her. He was content to just sit and wait for her to wake up on her own. He had a feeling Dr. Patience Forbes probably functioned most of the time on pure adrenaline and cheese puffs. She worked long hours and he doubted she ever got the sleep she really needed.

He frowned as he thought about her confession about her sexual experience in the shadow of a silo. How traumatic it must have been for a young woman to give her virginity to a young man so callous, so cruel.

Was it any wonder that she had trust issues? She'd had no family to nurture her and the one time she'd let down her guard it had been disastrous for her.

He wanted a family and she needed one, whether she knew it or not. But one picnic, one day in the fresh air wasn't likely to change her mind about her wants and needs and she was a woman who believed she needed and wanted nobody.

How could he want a woman who didn't believe in love? His growing feelings for her were those of a fool, but he didn't know how to stop himself from being a fool where she was concerned.

She slept for almost two hours and then shot up to a sitting position. "Oh my God, I'm so sorry." She shoved a strand of her shiny curly hair behind one ear. "How long have I been asleep?"

"About two hours," he replied. "And don't apologize, you obviously needed it."

"You must have been bored to death."

"Not really, I made up songs to the sound of your snoring."

She stared at him, obviously appalled until she saw his teasing grin. "You are so full of baloney," she said. "Even if I was snoring, Mac might be able to make up songs, but I'd bet songwriting is out of your repertoire."

He laughed. "You've got that right. I can manage a two-step for an impromptu barn dance, but I'm definitely not musically inclined. I've even been told that my singing closely resembles the sound of a bullfrog."

"I've never sung in front of anyone before," she replied. "But I have a feeling I'm not very good at it, either." She looked around and then back at him. "Should we finish packing up and go?"

"Probably. By the time we get back dinner should be ready." He stood and she did as well. They packed the remaining food and the plates they had used back in the duffel, leaving no trash on the property.

"I can't imagine being hungry again so soon." She picked up one end of the blanket and he grabbed the other. They folded it together and then he tucked it back beneath the saddle and fastened it and the duffel into place.

"It will take us a while to get back," he replied. "By then I'm sure you will have worked up an appetite again."

They were relatively quiet on the slow horse ride back. Once again his senses were all filled with her, the scent of her, the intimacy of his thighs pressed against hers, and his ever-growing desire for her.

She was the opposite of everything he wanted in

his future and yet she was the woman he wanted. Each and every moment he spent with her only confirmed that fact. She was going to break his heart. He felt it in his soul, in his very gut. She'd made no indication that she shared any of the same feelings for him that he did for her.

He would be her knight in shining armor while she was here at the ranch, protecting her from further harm, but when her work here was finally done she'd be headed back to Oklahoma City and a life that had no space in it for anything except her work.

The breeze blew a wave of loneliness through him. It was a familiar hollow air. Despite his friendships with his working cohorts, loneliness had chased Forest for the past several years.

He was thirty-two years old and ready to find a special woman and build a life with her. He was hungry for children and pot roast Sundays. He wanted more from life than to be a single cowboy humming the lonely blues, but he was certain that despite his growing feelings for Patience, she wasn't the woman who would fulfill his dreams.

He told himself it was enough that he keep her safe while she finished up her important work here. Hopefully when she was done she would unearth some clue that would point Dillon to the guilty.

By the time they got back to the stables and Forest unsaddled and stalled Thunder, it was almost five. "How about we head to our rooms and shower and by then we can get a bite to eat in the dining room," he suggested.

"Okay, although I'm not a bit hungry." They began the walk back to the motel.

"Once you smell whatever Cookie has prepared for the night I'm sure you'll be able to eat just a little bit."

She nodded and then stopped in her tracks. "I never saw who attacked me."

Forest stopped beside her and looked at her. Her gaze was distant and it was obvious to him she was accessing her missing memory from the night she had been attacked.

"I was walking back to my room from the tent and I thought I heard a whisper of sound behind me. I turned around once and didn't see anyone in the darkness. I'd only taken a couple more steps when I heard the sound again. But before I could turn I was hit in the head and that's the only thing I knew until I came to at the hospital." She sighed. "I didn't get a single glimpse of my attacker. I was hoping that once I remembered I'd have a memory that might help identify who it was."

She began to walk again, this time in quick, hard steps. "Patience." Forest hurried after her, recognizing she was angry.

She twirled around, her eyes narrowed. "What?"

"You're displaying anger and that's not what you're really feeling. If I was to guess—you're frustrated that you didn't see the attacker. You're frightened because you don't know who hit you or why. You're falling into an anger mode because that's safe and familiar to you."

She stared at him as if he was a steer with three heads. He tensed, expecting a full-blown explosion of temper from her. Instead she drew in a deep breath and blew it out on another deep sigh.

"For a man who has had very little formal education, you might be too smart for your own good. I am frustrated and more than a little bit scared, but anger is such a richer, more fulfilling emotion to dwell in."

"If you say so," Forest replied as they continued to walk.

"Don't you ever get angry?" she asked curiously.

"Not often and I try to save it for really important things, like a man beating on a woman or a kid, or somebody abusing an animal. That kind of crap makes me angry. It's just not an emotion I tap into very often. Do I get frustrated at times? Sure. Do I get impatient or irritated, absolutely."

"I go from zero to bitch in sixty seconds," she confessed.

He smiled at her. "I've noticed." By that time they had reached her room. "Thirty minutes okay with you?"

"That should be plenty of time," she replied. She unlocked her door. "I'll see you in thirty."

Forest waited to hear the door lock behind her and then he headed for his own room and a quick shower. As far as he was concerned, the day had been pretty near perfect. He'd managed to keep her away from her work and hopefully keep her brain moving at a slow, healing pace.

There was no way to keep her from returning to the blue tent tomorrow and he had no idea if her going back to her work would increase a danger to her or if her attack had been due to her angry words with the nasty ranch hands from Humes.

Realizing he hadn't heard from Dillon, he called the lawman as soon as he got into his room. Dillon answered on the second ring.

"Dillon, it's Forest. I was wondering why we haven't heard anything about the Humes men and their whereabouts when Patience was attacked."

"You haven't heard from me because I have nothing to report," Dillon replied, his frustration evident in his tone of voice. "The three men in question were alibied by several of their other coworkers for the night in question. Apparently there was an all-night poker game."

"Why am I not surprised," Forest replied dryly. "Whenever we have a fire set, fencing destroyed or an outbuilding damaged those men always alibi each other. They have more poker games than ranch dogs have fleas."

"And I've always tried to break those alibis," Dillon replied. "But they're thick as thieves and I can't get one to turn on anyone."

"Then we still don't know the who or the why of Patience's attack. She just remembered that when it happened she didn't see who did it. She was hit from behind and can't identify who did it."

Dillon released an audible sigh. "So that means everyone remains on my suspect list."

"Do you think I'm the wolf guarding the hen house?" Forest asked.

"I sure hope not. I figure that night you found her unconscious and drove her to the hospital if you'd wanted her dead, she'd be dead. You could have snapped her neck like a twig and nobody would have been the wiser."

Forest breathed a sigh of relief. The last thing he wanted was for the chief of police to believe he had taken on the guard duty of Patience to hurt her rather than to save her from any other approach of danger.

"I'm glad to hear that. You'll keep me informed if you learn anything?" he asked.

"I'll let you know anything I believe you need to know," Dillon replied.

Minutes later Forest stood under the shower and tried not to think about the fact that Dillon had everyone on the Holiday Ranch on his radar.

He shoved away the thought that any one of the cowboys here was capable of killing six young men in cold blood. Nor did he believe that anyone here would harm Patience in any way. He knew these men, he knew their hearts, their past hurts and there was no way he thought one of them was capable of this kind of violence against another person.

It was exactly thirty minutes later when he knocked on Patience's door. She stepped out of her room, and as always a spark lit up inside him at her mere presence in his company.

"Okay, I'll admit it. I smell something barbecue in the air and I'm ready to eat again," she confessed.

"Far be it for me to say I told you so," he replied with an easy smile.

They fell into step as they headed around the building to the dining room where they were greeted by the others who had already gathered for the evening meal.

Barbecue pulled beef on buns, coleslaw, baked beans and corn bread were on the menu and Forest was amused when Patience filled her plate with a little bit of everything.

"I don't know why I'm so hungry again," she said when they were seated in the same places at the same table as the night before.

"Fresh air and sunshine, they always build a healthy appetite," Forest replied. "Besides, there's nothing wrong with eating a good meal."

"You've had me eat more in a couple of days than I have in an entire month," she replied.

"And I'm proud of that," he boasted in return.

As always the dining room filled with laughter and talk of the day's work. Patience ate with a healthy appetite, and after dinner Mac picked up his guitar. Patience and Forest joined the others on the sofas to listen to the music.

They stayed later than they had the night before and when they left to walk her home, a brilliant pink sunset splashed across the sky.

"Thank you, Forest. I appreciate all the trouble you went to. It's been a nice day," she said as they rounded the building to her room door.

"It has been," he agreed. "And to top it all off we get a lovers' sunset to boot."

"A lovers' sunset?" She leaned against her closed door.

He gestured toward the western sky with its vivid pink color. "That's what we call a pink sunset around here."

"That's just a case of scattering," she replied. "It's the way air particles are…"

He didn't want to hear her scientific explanation about a beautiful sunset. He acted purely on instinct and the desire that had simmered through him for what seemed like forever.

He reached out, pulled her into his arms and took her mouth with his. He expected a slap or a full-blown temper tantrum from her but he was willing to take the chance. It was a chance worth taking. Instead of yanking away from him, she kissed him back.

She melted against him, her lips parting to allow him to deepen the kiss. Her mouth was hot and hungry against his. Her tongue swirled with his and then she abruptly broke the kiss and stepped back from him. Her back slammed into her door as her features radiated a stunned expression.

"I… I need to go." She pulled her key from her pocket and unlocked her door.

She was about to make her hasty retreat when Forest caught her by the arm. "I don't need scientific facts about what I see in the sky. It's a lovers' sunset, Patience, and that's all I need to know about it."

He released his hold on her arm and she escaped into her room, closing the door and locking it behind her.

Chapter 8

"I'm so glad you're feeling better," Devon said as he greeted Patience at the tent entrance the next morning. "I was worried about you, but everyone kept me up to date on your condition and it was obvious you were in good hands with Forest."

"Thanks, Devon, I'm fine and now it's time for us to get back to work and finish up this job as soon as possible." They stepped into the tent where she pulled on her white lab coat and Devon put on his.

She sat in front of her computer while Devon stood patiently nearby. He probably thought she was studying the picture in front of her of the burial site, but in truth she was attempting to find her focus.

It was true, she felt fine. Her headache was long gone and she was well rested, but she couldn't get that kiss with Forest out of her mind. It had been so unexpected and surprisingly welcome and wonderful.

That was the part that had her confused—the fact that she'd liked kissing Forest so much. Her brain was a bit muddied this morning.

She'd expected some awkwardness when Forest had appeared at her door to walk her to the tent that morning, but thankfully there had been none. He'd talked about the brief rainstorm that had moved through overnight and how little the storm had done to alleviate the dryness in the area.

By that time they were at the tent where she knocked on the trailer to signal Devon that it was time to get busy. Forest had walked to the corral where the horse awaited him.

"We're halfway through to the end of things here," Devon said, pulling her from her thoughts. "There are only three skeletons left to deal with. Maybe you should head back to Oklahoma City and let me finish up here."

She turned to look at him in surprise. Why on earth would he say such a thing? She was the official in charge of this site.

"Patience, I'm just thinking about your safety," he said. "I talked to those men who you met in the café and they all swore to me they had nothing to do with the attack on you. I believe them and that means somebody else, like maybe the killer, is after you."

She fought against the sudden quickening beat of her heart at his words. She was not going to be chased away from here by anyone until the job was done. "I started this work and I'll finish it. Besides, if the person who murdered these people kills me, when you take over for me you'll be his next target."

"But I'm a man and I have a gun." His brown eyes held her gaze steadily.

"Where did you get a gun?" she asked in shocked surprise.

Devon's cheeks flushed with unusual color and he reached up to straighten his glasses across the bridge of his nose. "It was given to me by one of the Humes men. I'd prefer you not mention it to anyone else. I'm sure it's illegal for me to have it, but I promised to give it back to him once our work here is done. I just wanted to make sure I was fully protected. I don't have a cowboy body-guarding for me."

"Where's the gun now?" she asked, still vaguely shocked that he'd gone out of his way to gain possession of a weapon. Did he even know how to use a gun?

"It's in the trailer."

"I'm assuming you know all about how to use it and normal gun safety." He nodded and she continued, "Don't worry, your secret is safe with me," she said.

After all, she couldn't blame him for wanting to protect himself if danger came his way, too. "We still don't know who was responsible for the attack on me. It's possible the person who killed these people is long gone from around here. Just be careful who you trust, Devon. I haven't heard any nice things about the men who work on the Humes ranch and my one encounter with a couple of them certainly didn't warm my heart."

"Don't worry, I can take care of myself. Like you,

I'm just eager to get this job done and get on to the next one."

"Then I guess it's time we get to work for real." She got up from the computer, and together she and Devon moved to the burial pit.

Only three more sets of bones to make into fully formed skeletons and then their work here would be finished. With three sets of bones already removed from the pit the others should go faster. She figured it would probably take no more than a day or two for each and then a final day to work up the last of her reports and turn everything over to Dillon.

Six or so days and then they would be pulling up stakes and moving on. Thankfully, they were almost at the end of the work instead of at the beginning. It was time for her to put the Holiday Ranch and specifically Forest behind her.

She had a feeling that if she spent too much time with him he'd manage to make her believe in all kinds of things that had nothing to do with facts.

He'd have her believing in lovers' sunsets and pot roast Sundays and love that lasted a lifetime. She didn't like it. His beliefs were in direct contrast to everything she had learned, everything she had experienced and been taught in her life so far.

She needed to get back to her apartment in Oklahoma City. She needed to be the angry shrew that kept people and any other scary emotions away.

She'd allowed herself to be vulnerable once and it had ended in disaster. Her father was right—emotions like anger and coldness kept people at bay, any other emotions were useless and made a person weak and vulnerable.

She shook her head to clear it from all thoughts other than those she needed to get the bones from the pit to the table. It should be a relatively easy day with just the three set of bones left.

Devon plucked the first skull from the pit. "Looks like all the others," he observed as he handed it to her.

She took it from him and noted the familiar injury in the back. Whoever had killed these young men had been consistent in the means of death. It took a lot of strength and a very sharp instrument to kill somebody in this manner.

"I heard that Dillon is interviewing all the cowboys both here and on the Humes ranch," Devon said. "He's definitely interested in the men here, especially since at the time Cass hired them on they were street kids who may or may not have used their real names, which makes it difficult for Dillon to check their backgrounds."

"They were all minors when they started working here. That fact in and of itself would make it difficult for him to get any real information about their pasts. But from what I understand, all the men here are using their real names, and he's already checked as much of their backgrounds as he can."

She leaned her hip against the fresh, empty table. "I've eaten in the cowboy dining room for the last two nights and have gotten to know the men a little better. It's hard for me to believe one of them is or ever was a killer."

"It was hard for people to believe Ted Bundy was a killer," Devon replied. "There are plenty of people who are always surprised to find out that their neighbor, their brother or their coworker is really a cold-blooded killer."

Patience didn't bother replying. He was right and there was nothing more to say about it. She weighed the skull, took photos and then made notes and then they were onto the next bone. The morning passed quickly and it was just after noon when she told Devon to take a break for lunch.

He left the tent and she sat in the chair next to the cooler and pulled out a soda. She wasn't going to step outside despite the stifling heat in the tent.

She refused to stand in the entrance and watch Forest at work. Yet at the same time she found herself rising from her chair and moving to the tent door. Her feet had definitely refused to listen to her brain.

There he was, in the corral with the horse. Dressed in his usual jeans and another white T-shirt, he looked strong and handsome with his black cowboy hat riding his head at a cocky angle. The horse was eating something out of his hand, and at the same time Forest used the other hand to stroke down the length of the animal's nose.

Apparently he'd managed to build trust with the horse. If she allowed it, would he be able to build a real trust with her? She didn't believe it was possible.

He definitely stirred her on a physical level. Her hormones were attracted to his. She couldn't deny the fact that she wanted him more than a little bit. The kiss they'd shared had only confirmed that her body wanted his.

Still, her world was science and his was not. He was a lonely man trying to replicate the family he had lost. If he thought she was somebody special to him, she had a feeling it was only because of her close proximity and the ease at which they had formed a relationship of sorts.

Before he could see her standing there watching him, she backed away and returned to her chair. She'd been seated there about thirty minutes when he appeared in the doorway, a small paper bag in hand.

"Is that lunch?" He gestured to the soda can she held in her hand.

"Along with my secret stash of cheese puffs in the cooler," she admitted.

"I figured the minute I turned my back on you that you'd return to your unhealthy ways." He held the bag out to her. "A ham-and-cheese sandwich that will go great with those cheese puffs of yours. I had Dusty get one for each of us from Cookie."

She stood and walked over to him and took the bag. "Thanks, but you don't have to take care of me every minute of every day," she said.

"I've never met anyone who needs taking care of more than you," he replied.

"Do you realize I'm a feminist?" She raised her chin.

He grinned, that charming slide of lips weakening her knees just a little bit. "Democrat, Republican, vegetarian or feminist, that doesn't mean I want to stop doing things for you. Besides, it's just a sandwich, Patience."

She'd been working up a head of steam, the self-protective anger that had served her so well in the past. But she couldn't get there, not with a sandwich in her hand and him looking so hot and sexy clad in his tight jeans and the T-shirt that stretched across his impossibly wide shoulders.

How could she be angry with a man whose eyes twinkled in merriment and sexy lips smiled at her with such natural charisma. "Thank you," she finally said. "You can go now," she couldn't help but add.

He tipped his hat and stepped back. "Yes, ma'am. Enjoy your sandwich and I'll be back to get you around five for dinner."

"I planned on working late," she protested.

"It's safer if you stop working early, eat in the cowboy dining room and are back in your room by dark. This isn't about your work, Patience. This is about how best I can keep you safe from any further harm."

She wanted to protest, but she was also aware of the sacrifices he was making for her. He was giving up his own routine and giving up time with his coworkers, with his friends, on her behalf. He had already done so much for her, more than she'd ever expected from anyone.

"All right, then I'll see you here at five," she finally agreed.

"And now I can go." He gave her one last teasing smile and then left to head back to the corral.

She returned to her chair and pulled the sandwich

from the bag. She was being spoiled by sandwiches delivered to her, by dinners with warm men and lots of laughter. She was being spoiled by Forest with his smiles and his thoughts about not just her safety but also her comfort.

Don't get used to it, a little voice whispered. This was all some sort of a surreal fantasy that had nothing to do with her real life.

She'd just finished eating when Devon returned to the tent to resume work.

The afternoon passed in relative silence. Neither she nor Devon was given to small talk. They only spoke bone language with each other.

What should have been a relatively easy job of piecing together the last three skeletons had become a confusing puzzle. They had three skulls left, but eight femur bones, indicating that the pit held at least the partial remains of four instead of three victims.

"Maybe the fourth skull is still buried in the pit?" Devon suggested after the surprising find.

"Maybe," she replied thoughtfully, although she didn't really believe it. The ground around the bones had been carefully excavated by her and Devon in the first couple of weeks when they had arrived at the ranch initially. Although the six skulls had immediately been evident, they had worked in grids to reveal any bones that might have been partially or fully buried by the shifting of dirt over time.

"I need to call Dillon." She glanced at her watch. It was almost four. She had a feeling she was going to be late for dinner.

It was almost five when Dillon finally arrived. He appeared in the tent entrance and paused, as if waiting for permission to enter all the way inside.

"Don't tell me more bones have disappeared again," he said.

"Okay, I won't," Patience replied. "You might as well come in and sit down." She gestured toward the folding chair next to where she sat. She'd already dismissed Devon to enjoy the cool comfort of the trailer.

"If you're inviting me to sit, then you must have bad news." He sank down in the chair next to her.

"You look exhausted," she observed. His eyes were slightly red, as if a good night's sleep was only a distant memory and the lines across his forehead cut deeper than usual.

"I've spent most of the day at the Humes ranch interviewing every person who worked there during the time of the crime. Although some of the men weren't working there during that time frame, they are mostly locals who lived in the area."

"Anything interesting come up?"

He frowned. "Nothing worth talking about. I think the answer to the identities of these victims lies with Francine Rogers, and she isn't due back from her cruise for another week. So, what bad news do you have for me?"

"We thought there were only three bodies left in the pit, but there are four, or at least part of four. We're missing a skull and I'm not sure what else at this point."

Dillon rubbed a hand across his forehead. "Are you sure?"

She bristled, but fought against her irritation at his question. "I'm positive. We have too many bones for only three bodies."

Dillon shook his head. "This case just gets more bizarre by the moment. Why would a skull be missing? This pit was buried beneath a shed, so I know there wasn't any animal tampering with the bones."

"And the dirt around the burial site was removed enough so that I don't believe it's buried and we just haven't found it yet," she added.

"So, potentially it could have been taken as a souvenir by the killer." Dillon rubbed a hand across his forehead as if in an attempt to ease a headache.

Patience nodded. "It would have been one of the first, if not the very first kill."

A shadow fell over the entrance as Forest appeared. "Problems?" he asked.

"You don't happen to have a skull hiding in your closet, do you?" Dillon asked ruefully.

"No skulls, not even a skeleton in my closet or anywhere else," Forest replied.

"We're missing a skull," Patience explained.

Forest frowned. "Was it stolen?" he asked.

"No way," Dillon replied firmly. "Since the incident with the bones being moved, I've had only my best men on duty here during the night. There's no way anyone got in here to steal a skull." He turned and looked at Patience. "So what does this do to you finishing up with the rest of the skeletons?"

"I won't really know until we continue on," she replied. "At this point I don't have a good feel for what's left in the pit. We've worked today on reconstructing victim four, but we know there are extra bones to indicate a victim we didn't know about before now."

Dillon rose. "You'll keep me informed on how the rest of the work progresses? We seem to be asking to keep each other informed on issues a lot lately."

"We do, but I'll definitely be in touch with any more news," she replied and also stood. She looked over at the gurney where she and Devon had been working before they'd discovered the additional femur bones. The other gurneys with the complete skeletons had been transported to Bitterroot's morgue where they were in cold storage until needed for further study.

They would be taken to the Oklahoma Crime Lab where an attempt to extract DNA and other more complicated testing would be done. Eventually they would be used as evidence in a criminal trial if anyone was charged with the murders.

"No more work for today," Forest said firmly. He obviously knew her well enough to know that she was reluctant to leave things so unsettled.

"No more work for me today, either," Dillon said wearily as the three of them left the tent. "I feel like I haven't had a good night sleep in over a month."

Dillon headed for his car and Forest fell into step with Patience as she walked toward her room to clean up for dinner.

"I guess this all just complicates things for you," he said.

"Yes, it does," she replied, her frustration obvious in the tiredness of her voice.

"I'm sure if given enough time you'll figure it all out," he said reassuringly.

She nodded. He had no idea how those extra bones only confused things. What he also didn't understand was that this new kink meant more time here and she knew that more time at the ranch, more time with Forest was dangerous on an emotional level for her.

She wanted to finish her work, but she was also emotionally afraid and far too vulnerable to the man who had appointed himself as her bodyguard.

Cassie was seated at the kitchen table eating dinner alone when Dillon appeared on the back porch. She opened the door and greeted him. "I saw your car parked down by the tent. Are there more problems?" She gestured him to the chair across from her at the kitchen table.

"This whole case is a problem," he admitted.

"Cup of coffee?" she offered.

"I see you're in the middle of dinner. I didn't mean to intrude."

"Nonsense, it's just a frozen dinner." She carried it to the counter and then poured them each a cup of coffee and returned to the table.

Dillon told her the latest news and as he talked, she tried not to notice the soft gray of his eyes, the way his dark hair was mussed in sexy disarray.

When he wasn't around she rarely thought about him, but whenever he was near she couldn't help the visceral attraction she felt for him, an attraction he obviously didn't feel for her.

In the months they'd been interacting, he'd been nothing but professional. She told herself that was a good thing: she definitely didn't want a relationship with the hot chief of police since she had no plans to make this place and Bitterroot her permanent home.

She was stuck here for the moment by the crime that had occurred on the property, but once that was all cleaned up, she was selling the place and returning to New York City where she belonged.

She was not going to be a Nicolette. She frowned as she thought of her best friend, the woman who had traveled with her young son and Cassie from New York City to the ranch when Cassie's aunt had been killed by the storm.

Nicolette had fallen hard and fast in love with Lucas Taylor, one of the cowboys working here, and before Cassie knew it, she and Lucas and Nicolette's six-year-old son, Sammy, had moved into their own house on a small ranch not far from the Holiday place.

In fact the two were getting married in a week and a half. When it was time, Cassie would be returning to New York City without her best friend and business partner.

Nicolette had traded her dreams of being a famous fashion designer for love. Cassie wasn't about to sacrifice her dreams of being a successful artist for anyone or anything. Never again, she told herself.

Heat leapt into her cheeks as she realized Dillon was staring at her expectantly and she had no idea what he'd just said or how to respond.

"I'm sorry?" she said.

"I asked if you and Adam had managed to dig up any employment records from around the time of the murders?"

"Yesterday we checked the outbuilding where Cass had stored a lot of old paperwork, but it was mostly financial items and bookkeeping stuff and some old diaries of hers. Unfortunately there were no employment records."

Cassie had retrieved several old diaries from the shed to read just to pass the long hours of the evenings, but she assumed they were mostly about ranch life and she hadn't started reading them yet.

Dillon sighed and took a drink of his coffee. "I somehow knew this wasn't going to be that easy," he said as he replaced his cup on the table.

"You look exhausted." Her fingers itched with a desire to stroke them across his furrowed brow, to brush away the strands of dark hair that had fallen across his forehead.

"I am," he admitted. He took another drink of his coffee and then stood. "And now I'm going to get out of here so you can finish your dinner."

"Thanks for stopping in and letting me know what's happening," she said.

"No problem. I'll be in touch."

She watched him leave and couldn't help but notice how his dark blue uniform looked so sexy on his broad shoulders and slim hips. Yes, she was definitely attracted to Dillon Bowie, but it was an attraction she would never act on. She wasn't meant to spend her life in Bitterroot, Oklahoma.

She thought of her foreman Adam. He was definitely showing signs of a real romantic interest in her, but she didn't reciprocate those feelings. Adam was a nice man and he'd been infinitely patient with her as he taught her about the ranch, but he didn't stir anything inside her like the crazy heat that flooded through her whenever Dillon was around. Thankfully Adam hadn't asked her out or anything like that, at least not yet.

She wanted neither man. She told herself she just wanted to get this crime scene cleaned up so she could get back to her life as a New York artist.

Chapter 9

It was Sunday after dinner and as Forest and Patience left the dining room, he asked her if she'd like to go on a horseback ride. "Just a short ride," he told her. "Maybe a little fresh air and evening sunshine will ease some of your tension."

"What makes you think I'm tense?" she asked with a curtness of tone that affirmed his assessment.

"You've been tense and wound up for the past couple of days, ever since you found those extra bones," he replied.

She sighed and shoved her hands in the pockets of her capris. "I thought I'd be finished by now, but these last set of bones aren't cooperating for me."

"Maybe tomorrow will be a more productive day," he replied. "Now…about that ride?"

She pulled her hands from her pockets and gave a curt nod. "Okay, since you won't let me go back to work tonight."

"You've worked enough for one day." They headed toward the stables. "You can start tomorrow with a fresh eye and a clear brain."

"My brain hasn't been clear since I realized there were four bodies still in the pit when I thought there was only three. We managed to put one back together over the last two days, but that still leaves two more and at least a partial one to go."

They entered the stable and she sat on a hay bale while Forest saddled up Thunder. Her anxiety had been palpable in the last two days. She moved with frenetic energy and she'd been overly quiet and distracted as if constantly trying to work out a puzzle in her mind.

She'd been distant with him, going from the dining room to her own room for the past two nights and foregoing any conversation or any real personal interaction.

Was it the bones that had her so disturbed or was it the kiss they had shared? A kiss he hadn't been able to forget and wanted to repeat again and again.

At least she'd agreed to the horseback ride, which would give them some time alone to talk and hopefully enjoy each other's company. For just a little while he wanted to take her mind off her work and into a place of peace.

Ten minutes later they left the stables with her ensconced in the saddle in front of him. As it had been with the last time they'd ridden together, her scent and her closeness nearly overwhelmed him. He would never grow tired of the scent of her, of the magic of having her close to him. It wasn't just a presumption on his part, it was a fact. She was in his blood.

A pang of pain pierced through his heart. She wanted to get her job done and leave here, and with each day that passed he wanted her more and she grew closer to being finished with her work.

He was on the precipice of falling completely in love with her, and despite knowing that he'd be left with a broken heart, he couldn't help the fall no matter how hard he tried.

She relaxed back against him as he headed Thunder in the direction of the pond where they'd had their picnic. It would be pretty at sunset with the last gasp of day reflecting on the water's surface.

"I guess you were right—this is just what I needed," she finally said to break the silence that had reigned since they'd left the stable.

"Good. I know you're upset by the way things are going in the tent, but you have to give yourself just a little bit of down time to escape the pressure," he replied.

They fell silent again as the ride continued, but he was pleased that she appeared to relax even more as Thunder carried them across the pasture. She fit in the saddle with him as if she'd been born to ride with him.

"I saw the horse eating something from your hand the other day," she said, breaking the silence.

"Apple slices," he replied. "She's coming along well. I'll be introducing her to some equipment in the next day or so."

"I always think of her as 'the horse.' Does she have a real name?"

"I've named her Twilight," he replied. "It's my favorite time of the day, and with her dark coloring I thought it was fitting."

"With her being so dark, you should have named her Midnight," she replied.

"Brody's horse is named Midnight, so I couldn't name her that."

"Brody...he doesn't seem like the friendly type."

"He likes to think of himself as a tough guy, but he's loyal and has a kind heart. You just have to dig through the macho-man facade to find it." Of course she wouldn't be here long enough to really get to know Brody or any of the other cowboys well enough to see just how big their big hearts were.

They reached the pond area and dismounted. He tethered Thunder to a nearby tree, and then they walked out on the wooden pier that extended over the edge of the pond.

He motioned for her to sit on the wood next to him. "Twilight is one of my favorite times of the day and this is one of my favorite places to spend it."

"Then you come here often?" she asked.

"Not often, but occasionally when I just need a little time away from the other men. It's a good place to sit and think and find peace. I'm not the only one of us who comes here to find time to be alone or to do a little spooning."

"Spooning?" She gazed at him curiously, her eyes a lush green in the evening light.

"Romancing. Don't worry, I didn't bring you here

to romance you. I just thought you might enjoy a little quiet time in a pretty place."

"Thanks." She pulled her knees up to her chest and wrapped her arms around them. "Why is it you seem to know what I need before I know what I need?"

He smiled. "Maybe I'm just more attuned to you than others have been before me."

"There was nobody before you," she replied and stared out to the water. "I've allowed you to get closer to me than anyone else in my life."

And still it wasn't enough to satisfy him. "Then I consider myself honored."

"Don't be. I don't have much to offer anyone. I work and most of the time I'm a shrew to anyone who might want to get close to me. That's just who I am at my core."

"I don't believe that," he replied. "I think like Brody you have something good and soft inside you."

She stared out over the water. "Don't be so sure. Are there fish in the pond?"

"Lots of fish. If you were going to be here longer, I could have brought you here to see how good you were at catching a big one."

She smiled and gave a slight shake of her head. "No time for fishing in my schedule."

They were quiet for a few minutes and then it was Forest who broke it. "Did you ever hear from your mother again after she left you and your father?" he asked, not wanting to process just how short her time here was growing.

She looked back at him. "No. I never got a phone call or a card in the mail or anything from her. No birthday or Christmas presents…nothing. We never heard from her again and then she was dead."

"Then you never really had any closure with her. I didn't have any real closure when my parents died, either. One minute they were in my life and the next minute they were gone. There was no time for goodbyes, no time to tell them one last time that I loved them."

Once again she cast her gaze away from him and into the distance. "My mother and I didn't share a relationship where I needed closure where she was concerned. I wasn't important in her life and therefore she wasn't important in mine." Despite her words Forest heard a faint vulnerability shimmer in her voice.

The conversation had grown too dark, too intense, and the last thing he wanted was to take her to a painful place in her past. "On a lighter note, my friend Lucas is getting married next Sunday, and I was wondering if you'd want to go to the wedding and reception afterward with me."

She turned and looked at him in surprise. "Why would I want to do that? I don't even believe in love and marriage."

"You don't have to believe in those things to enjoy the day," he countered.

"I don't even know if I'll still be around next Sunday. If my work is finished then I'll be gone."

"But if you are here, would you go with me? Lucas is a good friend and I'd hate to have to miss it." He was fully aware that he was using guilt to get her to agree, indicating that if she didn't go, then he couldn't attend either.

It was a blatant manipulation, but it was also the

truth. If she was still on the ranch then, there was no way he could attend the wedding and leave her here alone and unprotected.

"If I'm here, I'll go with you," she finally replied. "But I'm hoping to be able to finish things up in the next couple of days here."

"I can't lie, I'll be sorry to see you go," he admitted.

"Don't." She held up a hand to stop him from saying anything more. "I know where I belong and who I am and when it's time for me to leave, I won't look back." Her words held a definite warning to him.

"I know." His voice was soft, but hopefully he managed to mask his regret…his disappointment in knowing that within a month or two she probably wouldn't even remember his name. She'd be immersed in a new crime scene and living her life as she apparently always had…completely alone.

The sun dipped lower in the sky, shimmering gold and orange on the pond. "So beautiful," she murmured. "Thank you for bringing me here."

"You're welcome, and now we'd better head back," he said after a few minutes.

They both got up and left the small pier. "There's just one more thing I'd like to do before we go back." He knew what he planned was probably insane, but that didn't stop him from taking her hand and leading her into the shadow of one of the nearest corn silos.

"What are you doing, Forest?" Her eyes glittered overbright and her mouth trembled slightly.

"Hopefully, replacing a bad memory with a good

one," he replied. He pulled her into his arms and as she gazed up at him, he kissed her.

The kiss was deep and tender and once again he was surprised because rather than pull away from him, she melded against him and accepted, actively participated in the kiss.

He rubbed his hands up and down her slender back as she snuggled closer against him. Flames of desire stoked his insides, with the warmth of her body pressed so intimately against his own.

Still as much as he wanted to take their kissing and his caresses to the next level, that had never been his intention here and now. Reluctantly he released her and ended the kiss.

"You were broken in the shadow of a silo," he said softly and reached out and stroked his index finger down her cheek. "Now I hope that when you think of a silo, you'll remember a lonely cowboy's kiss instead of anything else." He dropped his hand to his side.

She immediately reached up and touched her cheek where his hand had been. "Thank you," she said in a mere whisper.

They didn't speak again as they remounted Thunder and began the long ride back. He'd touched her. He'd seen it in the glimmer of tears in her eyes and heard it in the tremor of her voice as she'd thanked him.

He hoped she'd remember the moment when a caring cowboy had kissed her with all the feeling that he had in his heart and soul, that the kiss alone would be enough to banish any terrible memories she still possessed of the shadows of a silo and a cruel college student.

He couldn't force her to be anything but the woman life had made her. He couldn't demand that she care about him as much as he cared about her. Unfortunately, he simply had to be ready to let her walk out of his life. He had to be prepared for the heartache he knew awaited him.

The sunset had transformed to the violet shadows of quickly approaching darkness. She leaned further back against him, as if exhausted by the day and maybe by the emotions he'd stirred inside her.

She believed she knew who she was at her core, but what she displayed to the world and what he'd seen of her were so different. He didn't have the tools to force her to see herself in her true light.

They were halfway across the pasture when the first shot rang out. The unmistakable whizz of the bullet passed inches by Forest's head.

Stunned, he acted purely on instinct. He jumped off Thunder and pulled Patience down with him. He hit the ground first, with her falling on top of him.

He immediately changed positions, rolling over on top of her as he fumbled to get his gun out of the holster. Another shot sounded and the bullet flew just over the top of their heads.

"Thunder...stable," he commanded. The horse responded immediately and took off at a fast gallop.

"What's happening?" Patience's terror laced her voice as she grabbed on to one of his forearms.

"Somebody is trying to kill us," he replied, not mincing words.

* * *

Patience trembled uncontrollably as yet another shot rang through the air, and the dirt near where they lay kicked up in a puff of imminent danger.

Forest returned fire, shooting toward the distance where the fencing separated Humes property from Holiday land. Large trees lined the fence, and with the darkness she knew Forest probably couldn't see the shooter.

She also knew whoever it was intended to kill her, but with Forest stretched out on top of her, he was the most at risk to take a bullet.

She'd wanted his protection, but she'd never truly considered that he would actually put his life on the line for her. It had all just been a theory in her head until this horrifying moment.

Her heart pounded so hard, so fast, she could scarcely catch her breath. A terror she'd never known before iced her through to her very bones.

She screamed as yet another bullet hit the ground far too close to where they hugged the ground. Forest muttered a curse as he returned fire.

"Dammit, there are too many trees and it's gotten too dark. I can't see the shooter," he exclaimed in frustration.

It was obvious the shooter could see them from his vantage point. Another sharp scream escaped her as she heard the distinct thud of a bullet into flesh and a faint moan issued forth from Forest.

"Forest!" Oh, God, he'd been shot. She tried to scrabble out from beneath him. She was the target and he'd been shot. It wasn't right. She couldn't allow him to be hit again. She should have never let him put himself in danger for her in the first place.

She struggled to get out from beneath him but he flattened his body against hers like a big boot on a small bug, making it impossible for her to move out from under him. "Lie still," he commanded.

"But you've been shot," she replied, tears of fear and anguish filling her eyes. How bad was it? Exactly where had the bullet struck him?

"I'm okay," he said tersely. He raised his head just enough to look around. "But we've got to get out of here. I think the shooter is up in one of those trees and we're sitting ducks here on the ground."

Before he'd gotten the entire sentence out of his mouth the night filled with the sound of pounding horse hooves. Like the cavalry riding to the rescue, Forest's fellow cowboys appeared in the moonlight.

"Check the trees along the fence line," Forest yelled out. "If anything moves, shoot it."

Five of the men on horseback headed for the fence while four of them formed a protective circle around Forest and Patience. Both Adam and Dusty jumped off their horses while the other two remained seated, their guns trained on the area where the shots had come from.

"Forest has been shot," Patience exclaimed in horror as tears coursed down her cheeks. "He's hurt. He needs help." Uncontrollable tears chased each other down her cheeks.

"I'm all right." He rolled off Patience and rose to his feet. The four horses surrounding them, along with the men checking out the area where Forest believed the shooter was, provided welcome safety.

"I sent Thunder back to the stable in case none of you heard the gunshots," he explained and helped Patience up from the ground. "Besides, I thought we'd be safer on the ground than on horseback. Obviously I was wrong. The shooter had to have been up in one of the trees to have such a clear shot at us on the ground."

"Let's get you both back to the rooms. Forest, you can ride my horse back," Adam said. "I'll ride with Dusty."

"And Dr. Forbes can ride with me," Brody Booth said.

It took only minutes to get everyone back on a horse and while the five men remained checking out the property line, the rest of them headed back to the rooms.

"Somebody needs to check Forest," Patience said to Brody. "I heard a bullet hit him. He's shot, but I don't know where." What if the bullet had struck him in the back? In a vital organ? What if he was already bleeding to death?

"He's a tough man. If he thought he needed immediate medical attention he would have said something when we all first showed up," Brody said. It was the last words they spoke until Brody eased her down from his saddle in front of her room.

Forest arrived and dismounted and in the dim light flowing from the room windows, Patience gasped at the sight of the blood trail that streaked down his left arm.

"You need Doc Washington to come out?" Brody asked him. He held the reins of both horses. Patience knew that Dr. Eric Washington had been around for years and was the last of the old-school doctors who still made house calls in cases of emergencies.

"No, I think it's just a graze. I'll get it cleaned up and I'm sure I'll be fine," Forest replied.

"Are you sure? Maybe we need the doctor," she said frantically. "Forest, don't be a tough man and just suck it up if you need a doctor."

"Believe me, I'll be fine," he assured her with a gentle tone.

Patience wasn't sure she would be fine. The sight of his blood horrified her. He'd been hurt because of her. She quickly unlocked her room door and took him by the hand. She needed to see for herself that he was okay.

"Come on, I'll clean you up," she said, still fighting tears that were a combination of residual fear and empathetic pain for him. Please don't make it bad, she prayed as she thought of his wound. Please don't let him be playing macho man when he's really been badly hurt.

He came with her willingly, and once they were inside her room she motioned him to the bed. "Take off your shirt," she said.

"I've been just waiting to hear those words from you," he said teasingly.

"Stop it. Don't make light of this. I don't like that. You could have been killed out there." A new tear splashed on to her cheek and before he could notice it, she whirled around and went into the bathroom where she had a first-aid kit stowed beneath the sink counter.

Her hand trembled as she reached for the metal case and another tear escaped from her. In theory the bodyguard duty that Forest had provided her had made her feel safe, but she'd never really processed that in his self-appointed job he might be hurt…or worse.

She swiped away the tear, wet a washcloth with warm water and then grabbed the kit and left the bathroom. Forest still sat on the bed, now without his T-shirt. The first thing she noticed was the wide, muscled chest that possessed not an ounce of fat. The second thing that drew her attention was the wound on the outside of his upper arm and the blood that oozed from it.

She released a silent sigh of relief. It was his arm, not his back, not his heart or any other vital organ. He would survive this.

Neither of them spoke as she quickly used the wet cloth to wipe away any blood that had flowed down his arm. She was grateful that the blood hid nothing but strong, tanned skin.

Once she had that cleaned up, she grabbed a small bottle of hydrogen peroxide and several cotton pads. "This might hurt," she said and began to dab at the wound.

"Don't worry, I can handle it," he replied.

"I'm not sure I can. I'm so sorry, Forest. I never wanted to see you get hurt," she said, once again fighting against a flood of tears.

"Don't apologize, it's not your fault. I was just doing my job and it was foolish of me to take you out on a horseback ride at this time of night. From now on we won't be taking any more rides away from here."

"That's fine with me." Gratefulness flooded through her as she saw that the wound was, indeed, a graze. No bullet had lodged in him; his outer arm might be sore for a few days, but no permanent damage had been done.

She cleaned the wound, added a liberal coating of antibacterial cream and then placed a bandage over it. It was only as she was putting on the bandage that she noted her intimate closeness to him.

She wanted to run a hand across the wide expanse of chest muscles and she remembered the searing kiss they'd shared by the silo before danger had appeared.

"You have a very gentle touch," he said, and his eyes held a wealth of emotions that instantly moved her back from him.

"Thank goodness it wasn't worse," she replied. "You could have been killed and it would have been all my fault."

"No, it would have been the shooter's fault," he countered.

Dillon and two of his officers appeared in her open doorway. "Adam called me," he said and eyed the bandage on Forest's arm. "Are you okay?"

"It's just a flesh wound." Forest got up from the bed. "Patience cleaned me up and it should be fine."

"Somebody tried to kill us," Patience said, shocked by the tremble in her voice. "Given what's happened in the past, I was probably the intended victim and Forest would have been collateral damage. You've got to get somebody under arrest for this. It was definitely attempted murder." Near hysteria brought her voice to a higher pitch.

"All of the men responded to the gunfire, so I'm certain none of the cowboys here had anything to do with the shots that were fired at us," Forest said and touched her arm as if to calm her.

"And they came from the ranch next door…the Humes place," Patience added. Hopefully the trembling of her insides didn't show on the outside. She couldn't stop thinking that if that bullet had struck Forest a couple of inches to the right, he would have been shot in the back. He might have been paralyzed for life or killed.

"The men are still out there seeing if they can find anyone," Forest said as he dropped his hand from her.

Dillon turned to the two men with him. "Go join the search and I'll get a statement here."

Forest sat back on the bed and Patience joined him there, leaving the chair against the wall for Dillon to sit in. As Forest recounted the moment of the first shot, Patience thought about the bones awaiting her, needing to distance herself from the terror of being on the ground and bullets slamming into the earth all around them.

It had been sheer luck alone that Forest hadn't been killed, and once he was dead whoever was shooting would have come after her. Initially, she'd wanted to hurry and finish her work here to escape Forest getting too close to her. Now she wanted to get done as quickly as possible so she could leave here and save his life.

It would be useless to try to talk him into stopping the bodyguard duty for the remainder of her time here on the ranch. He would refuse to leave her alone even more now that they'd endured a near miss.

Every minute that she spent on this ranch now put him at risk as much as herself. She'd never wanted to save anyone as much as she now wanted to keep him from harm. It was an alien feeling for her, to care about somebody's well-being.

Dillon finished up with his questions and then left to join his men out in the field. Forest remained seated next to her on the bed. "That was definitely a close call," he said. "Are you okay?"

"I'm fine." She was pleased by the strength of her reply. She didn't want him to know how frightened she was, how scary the whole incident had been.

"I just don't understand it," she continued. "I don't understand how anyone thinks killing me will stop the investigation into the murders."

Forest frowned. "I don't know. It's obvious we aren't dealing with a rational person. I still think it's probably the creep who murdered those young men and he's somehow attempting to protect a secret that you might uncover."

"What secret? So far the bones have yielded few answers," she replied. "When you first arrived here as a teenager you don't remember any other teens who might have disappeared?"

Forest shook his head. "Dusty and I were one of the last to arrive at the ranch. I don't remember any other young men here other than the ones who are still here. Besides, Dillon has already asked all of us that and nobody remembers any workers disappearing."

"I would imagine that not all of the Humes cowboys would have been working there at the time of the murders," she replied.

"True, but some were and others weren't working

on the ranch yet but were local teens from town," he replied.

She stared at the bandage on his arm, a faint nausea rising up inside her. "You could have been killed."

"Nah, my end of life isn't going to happen with me facedown in some cow field. I'm planning on dying peacefully in my sleep when I'm about a hundred years old. I'll have left behind a loving wife, children and dozens of grandchildren." He spoke lightly but with determination.

"You see your future so clearly." She tried not to focus on his magnificent bare chest but found staring into the beauty of his eyes equally unsettling.

He nodded. "I see it in my head. I dream about it in my sleep. What about you? What does your future look like?"

Before she could reply, Dusty appeared in the doorway. "Just wanted to check that you were really okay," he said worriedly to Forest.

"As you can see, Patience played nurse and fixed me right up," Forest replied. "It was just a little flesh wound."

"Thank God," Patience said, and Dusty nodded in agreement.

"The men are returning now. They didn't see anyone either on our property or on the Humes place," he said.

"I imagine the shooter ran off the minute all the men arrived," Forest said.

"Thank God you all showed up when you did," Patience said. She didn't even want to think of what might have happened if the Holiday gang hadn't arrived at precisely the moment they had. She and Forest had been sitting ducks in the open with no protection. Another minute or two out there all alone certainly might have led to tragedy.

Dillon showed up in the doorway once again. "We've checked everything out but with the darkness it's impossible to see much of anything. We'll be back here early in the morning to get a better look at things and see if we can locate the actual position of the shooter. Maybe we'll get lucky and he dropped his identification," he finished dryly. "I'll let you know what we find out tomorrow."

He left the room, as did Dusty, and then Forest stood. "It's late and I'm sure you're exhausted," he said.

She nodded, although she was far too wired to be exhausted. "Tomorrow I'll change your bandage and if it looks like the wound is getting infected then you need to see a real doctor."

"It should be fine." He picked up his T-shirt and then lingered at the door, as if reluctant to leave her. "Will you be fine for the rest of the night?"

"I'm not the one who got shot."

He cast her a gentle smile. "But you were the one who was terrified."

"I was, and I haven't thanked you for saving my life."

He tipped an imaginary hat. "All in a day's work, ma'am. I'll see you in the morning." He stepped out of the room and pulled the door closed behind him.

Patience walked over and locked the door and then leaned against it as myriad emotions roared through her. The abject terror of being shot at hadn't left her completely, nor had the fear, not just for herself, but for Forest as well.

The sound of bullets echoed in her head as the scent of the pasture earth filled her head. She raised a hand and placed it over her beating heart. Too fast. The rhythmic pounding was too fast to be normal.

She sank down on the edge of the bed and drew in several deep, steadying breaths in an attempt to calm the fear that still attempted to strangle her.

When she'd heard the thud of the bullet hitting Forest, she'd wanted to crawl out from beneath him and grab his gun. She'd wanted to kill the person who had shot him.

Somebody wanted her dead and they were willing to kill Forest if necessary to get to her. In her gut, in her very soul she believed it was the person responsible for the skeletons that had been unearthed.

Even though her death wouldn't stop the investigation, Forest had been right when he'd said that killers weren't always rational. If it was the person who had killed the young men in the pit, then she was the immediate threat and so the target. The killer would deal with the next threat when it came along.

It definitely made her wonder what she might find when she had all of the bones removed. Was there a definite clue in the skeletons as to who was responsible? Perhaps something in the pit itself?

She got up from the bed and headed for the bathroom and a quick shower. She stood under the warm water and thought of the kiss she had shared with Forest by the silo, remembered the sexiness of Forest's bare chest as he'd sat on her bed.

There was no question that he'd drawn her physically since the moment he'd had the audacity to step into her tent and introduce himself to her.

Hormones, she told herself as she pulled her purple nightgown over her head. Nothing more than raging hormones. She shut off her light and crawled into bed, but her mind continued to work overtime.

Forest kissing her, Forest's thighs against hers as they'd ridden on the horse, Forest with his charming smile and sexy eyes and physique. He'd thrown himself over the top of her to make sure she'd be safe. He'd been willing to sacrifice himself for her.

She wanted him.

She reminded herself it was probably a matter of hormones and the nearness of death that stirred such a roar of desire inside her now. But explaining it rationally didn't begin to satisfy it.

She didn't need to believe in love to want to be held in his big, strong arms. She didn't have to believe in a happily-ever-after to want his naked body close against hers.

Not wanting to overthink things, she got out of bed, grabbed her room key and left her room.

Chapter 10

Forest was in bed, clad only in his boxers and his bandage, but not sleeping when he heard the soft knock on his door. Assuming it was probably another one of the cowboys checking in to see that he was doing okay, he didn't bother pulling on jeans but rather left the bed and opened the door.

Patience stood just outside clad in her nightgown, the moonlight bathing her in a silvery glow. "Patience, is something wrong?" he asked, instantly tense and ready to spring into action if necessary.

"No. Can I come in?"

"Of course." He flipped on the overhead light, but as she entered the room she turned it back off.

"We don't need the light on," she said. She moved across the small room and into his single-sized bed.

"Patience, what are you doing?" His throat tightened as a new tension built up inside him. Lord, his arm ached from the gunshot graze, but seeing her in his bed set off a far different kind of ache.

"I just want to be here with you." Her tone of voice was softer than he'd ever heard it.

He remained by the door, confused about what exactly she wanted from him and afraid he might misconstrue the situation. "Are you afraid to be alone?"

"No, it's nothing like that. I just want to be close to you...intimately close." Her voice held a sexy rasp that he'd never heard before.

There was no way to misconstrue what she wanted, but still he hesitated. She'd been through a traumatic experience. Hell, they both had. Her presence here, in his bed, could only make him believe she wasn't thinking clearly. The last thing he wanted to do was take advantage of her and the situation.

"Patience, I know this has all been frightening for you," he began. "It was a bad night."

"That has nothing to do with what I want right now, and I want you." Her voice rang with a strong assurance that quickened his heartbeat and stirred a fire in his blood.

The bed was small, but she was like a butterfly pressed against the wall, leaving him plenty of room to join her. He'd wanted this, he'd wanted her, but he knew in his heart that what they were about to do was wrong for both of them.

That didn't stop him. God help him, but that thought couldn't stop him, for as he scooted onto the bed next to her she placed her hand on his bare chest. Her touch cast all notion of right or wrong straight out of his mind.

She leaned forward so their lips could meet, and her mouth tasted of the fire that had sprung to life inside him. She wound her arms around his neck and pulled herself closer…closer still to him. Her small breasts pressed against his chest as the length of her slender body molded to him.

The warmth of her, the nearness of her was like the dream he'd had night after night, and his mind could scarcely believe that this was not a dream, but rather a reality. She really was warm and willing and in his arms right here and right now.

Her tongue swirled with his as the kiss continued until she was gasping and he was gasping and yet neither of them seemed inclined to halt the kiss.

He finally tore his mouth from hers, only to rain kisses down the curve of her soft cheek and the line of her jaw. Her hands moved from his neck to caress his shoulders and across his back. She was careful not to touch the area around the bandage.

He'd imagined the touch of her hands on his bare skin so many times, but nothing had prepared him for the actual experience. Her hands were soft but heated, and each caress brought exquisite pleasure.

She sat up abruptly and he froze in position, wondering if she'd suddenly changed her mind about being here, about being with him.

His heart beat faster as in the semidarkness he watched her pull her nightgown over her head and throw it across him and to the floor below.

She wore no bra and her perfectly formed breasts begged his attention as she once again lay down beside him. His hands covered her breasts and he moved his thumb across her taut nipples.

"You are so beautiful," he whispered.

"You make me feel so beautiful," she replied and then gasped as his mouth took one of her nipples and he used his tongue to tease and torment the turgid tip.

She moved her hips into him, as if eager to have him take her, but he was in no hurry. Although she had him enflamed, he wanted to give her an experience to remember forever. He wanted her to be unable to forget this night with him when she finished her work and left the ranch. He wanted the memory of this night with him to be branded into her brain for the rest of her life.

He ran a hand down the flat of her stomach and touched the band of her panties. Cotton. He had expected nothing less from a no-nonsense scientist-type of woman. Still, he found them incredibly sexy.

She plucked at the waistband of his boxers, obviously ready for him to take them off. "Not yet," he whispered. "There's no rush. We have all night long."

"I don't know enough about all this to know what's a rush and what's not," she confessed.

The confession dug deep into his soul. Had she been with anyone since that one terrible time in college? Was he the first man in her life to truly want to make love to her for all of the right reasons?

If so, then she was a gift to him that he didn't want to abuse. He wanted her to experience the awe, the absolute wonder of a complete and thorough lovemaking.

He kissed her again, cupping her beautiful face with his hands. When he finished he gazed at her. "I'm going to ruin you for any other man."

"What do you mean?" Her eyes glowed in the faint light that drifted through the nearby window.

"I'll show you," he replied and then moved into action to do just that. He caressed and kissed her breasts until she mewled with pleasure. He kissed the freckles on her shoulders and then continued to stroke every inch of her silky skin except beneath and on top of her panties.

It took every ounce of his self-control not to strip off his boxers, yank off her panties and take her, but he never lost sight of his ultimate goal...to brand her as his with her pleasure unleashed.

When she was writhing on the bed, he finally moved his hand over the top of her panties and began to stroke her intimately. Her low moan and the thrust of her hips against his hand filled him with reward.

He increased the pressure and speed of his fingers. Her moans filled the room as she stiffened and trembled, release sweeping over her. She gasped his name. All tension left her body and she was limp beside him.

"That's just the beginning," he said and crouched over her and slowly pulled her panties down her legs and off her.

He brought her to climax again and only then did he take off his boxers. He gasped in surprise as she reached down and encircled his erection. She stroked him only a couple of times before his control grew to shatter-point.

He rolled to his back and pulled her on top of him,

allowing not only for the small bed space and the difference in their size, but also to let her be in charge from this moment on.

And she took control. She lowered herself onto him and when he was surrounded by her moist heat, she leaned forward and draped herself against his chest.

They remained locked together but not moving for several achingly long moments. He stroked the silkiness of her hair, and she turned her head so they could share a kiss. Then she began to move her hips against his.

Intense pleasure ripped through him and a deep, low moan escaped him. She sat up and threw her head back and increased the depth with which she took him in. He struggled desperately to maintain control, to hang on so that they could finish together.

Then she was there, her muscles contracting around him as she shuddered, and he let go and groaned with the intensity of his climax.

When the shudders had stopped, she collapsed on him and then rolled to his side. He wrapped an arm around her to keep her from falling off the small bed.

"Is it always like that?" she asked softly.

"Only with me," he replied.

Her breathing slowed, as did his. He curled around her back. Within minutes he was surprised to realize she'd fallen asleep.

He tightened his arm around her and breathed in the sweet scent of her hair. He already wanted her again… and again. He didn't just want her for a night or two in this room.

She was the woman he wanted as his wife. Heaven

help him but Dr. Patience Forbes was the woman he wanted for the rest of his life.

Patience awoke just before dawn. The deep, even breathing coming from Forest indicated that he still slept. She didn't move, not even a muscle. Instead she allowed herself to just experience the novelty of being in bed with a man. Not just any man, but with Forest.

His body was warm against hers and with his arm slung across her middle, it was as if she were a precious treasure he feared might accidentally fall to the floor and break.

Safe. She'd never felt so safe, so cared for in her entire life. Warmth suffused her as she remembered the night before. She'd expected a quick and uncomplicated bout of sex. But he'd given her so much more. She'd had no idea it could be so...so wonderful.

She suddenly felt the need to run, to escape thoughts of sex with him, to forget the tender, heated caresses, the depth of emotion that had glowed in his eyes as they'd joined together as intimately as two people could join.

Still, despite the impulse to escape, she remained unmoving, reluctant to awaken him. With her safe in his arms this was probably the best sleep he'd gotten since he'd taken on the job as her personal bodyguard.

It had just been sex. Awesome, but just sex, she assured herself. There was no reason for things to now get weird between them.

She wasn't on birth control and they hadn't used a condom, but she wasn't particularly worried about unintended consequences. Her cycle was in a place where pregnancy shouldn't happen.

She wasn't the woman to give him children, to believe in his dreams. This had just been sex without any emotional ties. She closed her eyes once again and tried to pretend that she hadn't seen his heart in his eyes, that his kisses hadn't been filled with an emotional depth.

Just a few minutes later Forest stirred, and she quickly slid out from under his arm and off the bed. "Good morning," he said.

"Good morning," she returned and grabbed her nightgown off the floor. She pulled it on over her head and searched the floor for her panties.

"In a hurry?" His voice held a sleepy sexiness that tempted her to jump back into the bed.

She glanced at him. He was all sexy hunk with his dark hair tousled and the sheet at his waist, exposing his muscled chest. She went back to the panty hunt. "I need to get back to my room before somebody sees me leaving yours."

"Ah, trying to avoid the walk of shame."

She found her panties and stepped into them. "I'm not ashamed of what we did. It was just sex between two consenting adults."

She could swear he flinched slightly at her words. "Just a crazy chemical or whatever reaction between us," he said.

"Exactly." She opened his door and grabbed her room key from the top of the nearby chest of drawers. "I'll be ready to get to work in about two hours, when the sun is up and I have plenty of light."

"I'll be at your door in two hours." He didn't move from his position on the bed.

She went into her room and headed for the shower. As wonderful as the sex had been, she needed to wash away the scent of him that lingered on her body. She wanted to forget the whole night because thinking about it would give it more importance than she wanted.

It was even more important now that she finish her work and leave. She needed to put this experience… and Forest behind her. Forest with his lovers' sunsets and dreams of love and family. She'd allowed him far too close to her.

She didn't want to break his heart, but feared he'd already developed feelings for her that would never come to fruition because she didn't believe in "feelings."

As much as she wanted to finish and leave the Holiday Ranch, for the next four days she and Devon worked but couldn't finish up the job.

It was Saturday afternoon when Forest stepped into the tent entrance and told her she'd been summoned by Cassie to the big house.

"Why does she want to see me?" Patience asked Forest as they left the tent. "I've hardly spoken to the woman at all since I arrived here. I've turned down all of her invitations to join her for dinner. I have nothing to say to her."

"I'm sure she wouldn't want to see you unless it was something important," Forest replied.

They fell silent as they continued to walk. Since the night she had gone to his room and they'd shared intimacy, she'd maintained her distance from him as much as possible.

She still ate dinner in the cowboy dining room each evening, but after eating she immediately retired to her room where she read her tabloids and indulged in other people's lives from a safe distance.

She couldn't imagine why, after all this time, when she was at the end of her job Cassie would want to interact with her now. But it hadn't been a simple invitation to meet her at the big house. It had been more of a command.

She probably wanted to get an up close and personal idea of how soon they would be finishing things up and getting off her property. Nobody wanted to look out their window day after day and see a crime scene tent in their backyard.

The ranch house was a huge, attractive two-story with a wide back porch, and it was to the back door that Forest led her. He knocked and Cassie immediately answered, a bright smile on her pretty face as she gazed at Patience.

"Dr. Forbes, please come in," she said. She looked at Forest. "Why don't you give us an hour or so?"

He nodded and turned and walked away. Patience stepped into a huge kitchen and fought a case of nerves. Why on earth would Cassie want to talk to her for a whole hour? What could they possibly have to chat about?

"Would you like a cup of tea or maybe something cold to drink?" Cassie asked.

"No, thank you. I'm fine." Just curious and more than

a little bit nervous, Patience thought. Other than a few female coworkers, Patience had shared very little time with other women.

"Then please come in and sit. I'd like to discuss something with you." Cassie gestured her into a great room with comfortable dark brown leather furniture and windows that looked out on the pasture and outbuildings in the distance.

Patience perched on the edge of a leather chair and Cassie sat on the sofa facing her. "I understand that you're going to Lucas and Nicolette's wedding tomorrow with Forest," Cassie said.

The wedding. Patience had forgotten all about it. When she'd agreed to go with Forest, she'd planned on already being gone. Now, if she didn't go with him, he'd stay here with her and miss his friend's big day, and that wouldn't be right after all that he'd done for her.

"Yes, I guess I'm going to the wedding as Forest's guest," she finally replied. She would suck it up and go with him because he deserved the day spent among his friends and sharing in the special occasion.

Cassie tucked a long strand of her shiny blond hair behind her ear. "I don't mean to be indelicate here, but I was wondering if you had something to wear?"

Patience stared at her, stricken by the fact that she hadn't even considered having something appropriate to wear to a wedding. "I'm not sure that my lab coat and capris would make the right statement. Is there a store in town where I could buy something before tomorrow?" she asked worriedly.

Cassie smiled. "Bitterroot is great if you're looking

for a new pair of cowboy boots or a plaid flannel shirt, but it doesn't offer much in the way of semiformal wear. Most of that kind of clothing is either special-ordered in or women go shopping in Oklahoma City."

"I don't have time to go to Oklahoma City," Patience said more to herself than to Cassie. Making such a trip would take a huge chunk of time out of her day, time she needed to continue her work.

"Never fear, I've got you covered. Upstairs I have several dresses I've never worn because I got them for a ridiculously low sale price and bought them even though they were a bit too small for me. You know, I depended on losing those five pounds that as of yet haven't gone away and probably never will. One of them should fit you perfectly."

"Oh, I couldn't," Patience protested, even though she had no real alternative.

"Of course you can," Cassie replied and jumped up. "Come on, let's head upstairs and raid my closet. It will be fun."

Reluctantly Patience got up and followed behind Cassie as they climbed the stairs. Why was this virtual stranger being so nice to her? Why had everyone on the ranch been so nice when she could be such a disagreeable witch?

Cassie led her into a large bedroom with an adjoining bathroom that was obviously the master suite. "When my best friend, Nicolette, and I packed to come here I had no idea what to expect, so I filled my suitcases with formals, semiformals, silk slacks and blouses." She shook her head and smiled. "I had no idea what I was getting myself into becoming an Oklahoma ranch owner."

She opened her closet door. "Since then I've added an array of appropriate ranch clothes to my collection." She scooted clothes aside and reached to the very back and pulled out several short dresses that still had tags hanging from them.

"I'm small, but you're even smaller, so one of these should fit you just fine. Why don't you try the silver and black one on first and then the lavender. Leave the mint green dress for last." Cassie moved to the door. "Call me when you're ready so I can see each one of them on you and we can make a final decision." She left the room and closed the door behind her.

Patience ran a hand down the silk material of the beautiful black-and-silver short-sleeved dress. She'd never worn anything as gorgeous as any one of the dresses on the bed.

She knew the wedding was planned for five at the Methodist Church in Bitterroot and at six there would be a reception at a nearby community center.

Knowing she had no real options, she quickly removed her blouse and capris and pulled on the first dress. "Okay, I'm ready," she called through the door.

Cassie entered and eyed her critically. "The length is all right, but it does nothing for your beautiful skin tone and it's a little big in the boob area. It would do in a pinch, but let's see how the others look on you." Once again she left the room.

Patience took off the dress and slipped on the next

one. The lavender was proclaimed by Cassie to be too long and just not right.

The sleeveless mint green dress felt right the moment Patience pulled it on. It was a tiered chiffon that seemed to float around her yet emphasized her petite shape.

Cassie clapped her hands together at the sight of her. "I just knew this would be the one," she exclaimed. "And now for shoes." She bent down in the bottom of her closet and pulled out a pair of silver high heels. "These should work. Try them on." Patience stepped into the heels and found them a perfect fit.

"And now, a nice set of silver earrings and some makeup and you'll be good to go." Cassie pulled out a plastic bag from one of the drawers and tossed it on the bed in front of Patience.

She opened it to find a new tube of pale pink lipstick and mascara and a tasteful dangle of never-worn silver-tone short earrings. She looked up at Cassie in surprise. "Did you plan all of this?"

Cassie sat on the edge of the bed, appearing pleased with herself. "I was in town yesterday and thought about you. I figured a woman who digs around in the dirt and works with old bones probably hadn't brought with her much of anything to go to a social event."

"I swear I won't spill a drop of anything on the dress and I'll pay you back for the other things."

"Nonsense, it's all my gift to you, including the dress and the shoes. Besides, no matter how much I starve myself I'll never get into that dress, and it looks so lovely on you."

Patience blinked away a sudden burn of tears. Jeez,

something about this ranch and the people here affected her on a level she'd never experienced before. "Why? Why would you be so kind to me? I've scarcely given you the time of day since I've been here."

"You've been working. I understand that you haven't been here to socialize. In the short time I've been in Bitterroot I've learned that this is what the people here do…they help each other in times of need. Besides, I know how much you mean to Forest and that tells me you're a wonderful person."

Cassie stood. "And speaking of Forest, he should be back here in a few minutes. I'll just get out of here so you can change back into your regular clothes."

Minutes later the two women went back down the stairs. The beautiful green dress was hung and covered with a white cleaner bag. The shoes and other things were in a separate bag.

"I don't know how to thank you," Patience said when they reached the kitchen. "I could write you a check for everything."

"Don't offend me by taking away my joy at giving you a gift. You can pay me back by having a wonderful time tomorrow with Forest. Forget all about work and murder and enjoy the atmosphere of love and friendship." Cassie looked toward the back door. "And look, here comes Forest now."

The two women said their goodbyes and then Patience left the house to meet Forest. "Did you have something to do with the Cinderella moment that just happened with Cassie?" she asked him with suspicion.

"I might have mentioned to her in passing that I

wasn't sure what kind of clothes you'd brought with you," he replied. "I can't have my date showing up to my friend's wedding in a pair of shorts and a T-shirt."

She wanted to be mad at him, at Cassie and at everyone who had shown her such kindness. She wasn't used to people treating her so nicely. She wasn't accustomed to anyone caring. She didn't like it because it was just a little bit scary, because deep in her heart she knew she really didn't deserve it.

Forest tugged on the black tie that threatened to strangle him. The last time he'd put on a suit and tie had been for Cass's funeral.

He didn't want to think about that somber, heartbreaking occasion now. Besides, Cass would have been thrilled to see one of her "boys" getting married and moving on with his life.

Today was all about joy and love and he couldn't wait to spend time with Patience away from the ranch. Beneath his suit coat he wore his gun, aware that anytime they were out in public together danger could find them. He wasn't expecting trouble, but would be ready if it came knocking.

Hopefully today nothing would happen but good times. Since the night he and Patience had made love, there was no question that she'd tried to distance herself from him, but that only made him suspect it had meant much more to her than she'd pretended or wanted to admit to herself.

She'd said it was just sex, but whether she knew it or not, she'd made sweet, hot love with him. Even in the last couple of days as she'd attempted to gain distance, her gaze had lingered on him for seconds too long, she'd touched him more frequently…casual but meaningful from a woman he knew didn't touch others often, if at all.

She might not believe in love, but that's what emanated from her whenever they were together. She might be fighting the feelings, but they were there, and he hoped that by the end of today she'd be more open to them and to him.

There was nothing like being surrounded by love to feel it in your heart, in the soul. Lucky Lucas, he was getting his dream. He was marrying the woman he loved, adopting Nicolette's young son and working on his own ranch.

It was what Cassie had wanted for them all, to grow into men who would learn to trust again, learn to love and build families of their own. She would definitely be smiling down from Heaven today.

He moved his arm, grateful that the bandage had come off and the bullet graze was nearly healed. He doubted he'd even have a scar. The only scar he might harbor was the memory of that moment when he believed he'd be killed, leaving Patience vulnerable to the same fate.

At four-fifteen he left his room and knocked on Patience's room. She opened the door and his breath caught in the back of his throat. The green dress matched the hue of her eyes and brought out the splendid red of her hair.

Silver earrings danced at her dainty ears and her lips

were pink and her eyelashes sinfully long and dark. "You look absolutely stunning," he said when he finally found his voice.

"So do you," she blurted and her cheeks flushed with color. "I mean you clean up real nice for a cowboy."

He chuckled and took her room key from her and shoved it in his back pocket. "Your chariot awaits," he said and gestured toward the navy pickup with silver trim. "Sorry it isn't a limo, but you don't find too many cowboys with luxury rides."

"The ride doesn't matter, it's the company that counts," she replied and headed for the passenger door.

Was she even aware of her own words? Of the confirmation that she wasn't as immune to him as she wanted him to believe? He gave a small shake of his head and climbed into the driver's seat. She had no idea that she kept his brain muddled with confusion most of the time.

She kissed him as if she meant it. She'd made love to him with passion and when she looked at him he saw something more than mere affection flickering in the depths of her gorgeous eyes. Was he merely seeing what he wanted to see? He shoved away any confusing thoughts and focused on the evening to come.

"Happy is the bride that the sun shines on," he said once they were underway.

"It is a beautiful day," she replied.

"I hope you manage to put your skepticism aside about the whole love and wedding thing for the rest of the evening." He cast her a sideways glance.

"I don't know about that, but I promise I won't mention my skepticism to anyone. So, what should I expect from this ceremony and reception?"

He gave her a surprised glance. "You've never been to a wedding before?"

"I don't socialize enough to have ever been invited to one before."

"Well, darlin', your socializing habit is about to change."

He felt her gaze lingering on him. "I might change my habit for a night or two due to unusual circumstances, but people don't change who they are at their core and the beliefs they have."

"You'd be amazed what love can do," he replied firmly. "It was Cass's love that brought us all together and made us men, and believe me that wasn't an easy task. Most of us were wary and broken and not in a place to trust or care about anyone. Her love healed wounds that for most of the cowboys at the ranch ran soul-deep."

She leaned back in the seat and didn't reply. Instead she gazed out the passenger window and the silence between them grew.

What was she thinking? How he wished he could crawl into her mind and not only see her thoughts, but also erase the childhood and her traumatic college experience that he believed had made her into a woman afraid to trust, afraid to even believe in love.

He'd managed to work his magic on the horse, but he had such little time left to do the same with Patience, if it was even possible to change her beliefs.

The church parking lot was almost full, the prevalent

type of vehicle in the spaces being pickup trucks. All of the men from the ranch had been invited. Adam Benson was Lucas's best man, and Cassie was Nicolette's maid of honor. Forest assumed they had already arrived.

It wasn't just people from the ranch who had been invited to the special event. There were men and women from other ranches as well as townspeople. Thankfully nobody from the Humes ranch had received an invitation.

He found an empty parking space and pulled in, then hurried from the driver door to the passenger side to help Patience out of the truck.

"Looks like they have a big crowd," she said when they walked toward the front door of the quaint white building with a tall steeple.

"Both of them have lots of friends, although the wedding itself is small. Cassie and Adam are the sum of the wedding party, except for little Sammy who is serving as ring bearer."

She reached for his hand as they walked up the two steps to the front door. The gesture both surprised and delighted him. She was apparently a bit uneasy about mingling with a crowd of people. Her grasping his hand surely meant she considered him a source of comfort.

There was no bride side and groom side of the pews. Neither Nicolette nor Lucas had family to attend. As Forest and Patience walked down the center aisle to find a seat on one of the pews, Forest was greeted by many townsfolk who had been invited to share in the festivities. Disappointment flooded through him as Patience finally dropped her hand from his.

"That's Daisy Martin," he murmured as he waved a hand toward a plump woman with flaming red hair. "She owns the café. Next to her is Trisha Cahill, the waitress that Dusty has a huge crush on."

They finally sat next to the aisle five pews back from the front of the church and Forest continued to point out people to her. He leaned toward her, filling his senses with the familiar, sweet scent of her. "Right next to me is Fred Ferguson who owns the motel and next to him is Janis Little, a waitress at the Watering Hole."

"The Watering Hole?" She looked at him curiously.

He grinned. "The bar where every self-respecting cowboy goes to get lit and play a little pool."

"Do you go there often?"

"Occasionally, but I'm not much of a drinker. I'm usually the designated driver and corral all the drunks to get them home safe and sound."

She placed a hand on his forearm. "You're a nice man, Forest. You deserve all of your dreams coming true."

You are my dreams. The words were on the tip of his tongue, but at that moment organ music filled the church, the minister took his place and Lucas appeared next to him.

Lucas looked handsome in his black tux and pale pink bowtie and cummerbund. He also appeared nervous as he shifted his weight from one foot to the other and stared down the aisle, not making eye contact with anyone in particular.

Forest grinned inwardly. Lucas had confronted a killer to save Nicolette from danger when she'd first arrived in town with Cassie. He'd wrestled steers and faced hungry wolves among the cattle without blinking an eye. But he stared down the aisle and fidgeted with his tie as if deathly afraid his bride-to-be might not show up.

Forest had seen the love that had blossomed between the two and the young boy who was so hungry for a father figure. He knew there was no way Nicolette wouldn't be at the altar within a matter of minutes.

Six-year-old Sammy appeared carrying a white pillow with two rings attached. He walked slowly and deliberately halfway down the aisle and then broke into a run and leapt into Lucas's arms.

The crowd laughed and ahhed and a deep yearning swelled up in Forest's chest. What must it be like to have a child who loved you unconditionally? He wanted that. He wanted the child and the loving wife to go with a baby.

He glanced at Patience. Her eyes shone overbright, as if she were fighting back tears. The dragon lady definitely had a soft center and nobody knew that more than Forest. If he could only dig deep enough to convince her that love wasn't just a kiss or simple sex. It was the breath of life.

The Wedding March began and everyone got to their feet. Without looking backward, Forest knew the moment Nicolette stepped into view, for Lucas's features lit with a happiness, a force of love that was palpable.

Lucas hugged Sammy and set him on the floor next to him, then watched intently as Nicolette, clad in a soft pink wedding gown, approached him. She had probably decided to forego the traditional white because this was her second marriage.

When she passed their aisle, there was no denying the serene happiness that she radiated. She was a woman certain of what she was doing and the man she was about to bind herself to for the rest of their lives.

Once Nicolette had joined the others, the music stopped and everyone sat back down. When they spoke the vows they had written themselves, the only sound was the sniffle of women crying tears of joy and the ring of the couple's love for each other.

He glanced again at Patience. It had appeared she was on the verge of tears before, but now she had her arms crossed and her chin up, as if daring anything happening to affect her in any way.

Rather than be discouraged, he was encouraged. Her defensive posture meant she felt threatened, and if she felt threatened it was because something in the setting, in the ceremony and the collective love in the room was touching her on an emotional level.

It was just after five-thirty when the minister introduced the new couple as Mr. and Mrs. Lucas Taylor and their son, Sammy.

"Now I got a real dad," Sammy exclaimed. Everyone whooped and cheered as Lucas picked Sammy up in his arms and the three of them headed down the aisle to leave the church.

If Patience's beliefs had been threatened during the simple ceremony, then he hoped the reception shook her to her very core because before she left the ranch, he intended to proclaim his love for her.

Chapter 11

Patience would never admit to anyone how much the wedding ceremony had touched her. She believed love didn't exist, and yet it had been difficult to look at Lucas and Nicolette and not believe that that kind of strong emotion wasn't what they felt for each other.

"It was a nice ceremony," Forest said as they drove the short distance from the church to the community center. He shot her a quick glance.

"It was okay for people who believe in such things," she replied.

She thought he expelled a small sigh. "The reception should be fun. Cookie catered the food so I know it won't be the usual after-wedding little cakes and dainty sandwiches. I also heard they hired the Croakin' Frogs band for the night, so there should be plenty of foot-stomping music."

"The Croakin' Frogs?" Dear Lord, what had she gotten herself into?

"It's a five-piece country Western band. They play a lot of places around the state and are building a decent following. Scott Earnhart is the lead singer and lives here in Bitterroot. Expect lots of dancing and eating and laughter."

"You told me you sing like a frog. I'm surprised you aren't their lead singer," she replied teasingly.

He laughed, that low deep rumble that had become so familiar, so welcome to her ears. "I croak off-key," he replied.

He looked so handsome in his suit, white shirt and black tie. His hair was neatly combed, and she was slightly amused that instead of dress shoes he had on a pair of highly polished black cowboy boots. You could take the man off the ranch, but you apparently couldn't take the cowboy from the man.

She turned her head to look out the window. She was definitely out of her comfort zone, but she'd been out of her comfort zone since the moment Forest had introduced himself to her.

It had all seemed so easy with him, their conversations, their time spent alone and among others. Their relationship had felt organic, as if neither of them had worked hard for it, but it had sprung to life on its own.

For the first time she realized how lonely her life had been before him, how isolated she'd kept herself from fun and laughter and friendships that wouldn't have taken away anything but might have added a richness to her life.

It was a stunning self-realization, and before she could give it any deeper thought they'd arrived at the community center.

The one-story building itself was huge and painted white with a cheerful sign announcing it to be the Bitterroot Community Center. It sat in the center of a large lot that provided plenty of parking. A smaller sign just outside the front door announced Friday night bingo games and a monthly meeting of the Bitterroot Women's League.

Inside, a stage was at the back of the large room, and the band had already set up in preparation of their performance. A highly polished wooden dance floor was right in front of the stage.

A head table was covered with a pink tablecloth and held a centerpiece of pale pink and white flowers. Five chairs were behind it for the newlywed couple, Cassie and Adam and Sammy.

A buffet was set up along one long side wall, and the center of the room held round tables covered in light pink tablecloths and with white candles in silver holders as centerpieces.

"Let's grab a table near the dance floor," Forest suggested and took her by the elbow to guide her forward. Each table sat eight, and by the time the room had begun to fill, Dusty, Sawyer, Clay and Flint had joined them, with Clay's date, Ramona, and Flint's date, Julie Hatfield, who was a waitress at the café.

It was a full table and slightly daunting, as Patience didn't know Flint or Clay very well and both of the women were strangers.

Thankfully, Julie and Ramona were friendly and talkative, and as they ate they regaled Patience with stories about the people in town, the cowboys on the Holiday Ranch and then asked her easy-to-answer general questions about her work.

By the time the band began playing and Patience watched Lucas and Nicolette share the first dance, she was relaxed and looking forward to a dance with Forest.

Forest teased Dusty, challenging him to ask Trisha, who sat at another table across the room, to a dance. Instead Dusty stood and took Patience's hand. "Come on, Doc. Let me have a dance with you before the big ox takes control of you."

Patience laughed and allowed Dusty to lead her out on the floor. Maybe it was the two glasses of champagne she'd consumed a bit too fast, or maybe it was just the atmosphere of caring and acceptance that allowed her to shrug off some of her inhibitions.

Once she was on the floor, she found herself in the arms of one cowboy after another. She not only danced with all of the other cowboys from the Holiday Ranch, but also with Dillon and Fred Ferguson, the motel owner.

She finally returned to the table, exhausted and yet still filled with a bit of adrenaline from the fun. Forest took a sip of his glass of water and eyed her in amusement.

"Cinderella is the belle of the ball," he said in amusement.

"Except for with you," she replied. "You haven't danced with me yet." He was the man she most wanted to dance with, the person she wanted to pull her close and wrap her in his big, strong embrace.

"I figured you should save the best for last," he replied, a wicked little gleam in his eyes that heated her from head to toe.

"And you're the best?" she asked teasingly.

"The best you'll ever have," he replied with a confidence she found breathtakingly sexy.

His words instantly evoked memories of their lovemaking. No, she mentally corrected, not lovemaking. Sex. It had just been sex between two adults who had been pulled together by hormones and body chemistry that had called to each other.

Her thoughts were interrupted by a couple stopping by their table to visit with Forest. It had been apparent to Patience the moment they'd walked into the church that Forest was not only liked and respected on the ranch, but among the townspeople of Bitterroot, as well.

He'd come to the Holiday Ranch as a heartbroken teenager in mourning for the parents he'd lost. He'd had lived a tough life on the streets and yet had turned into a caring, honorable man. She'd told him people didn't change, and yet he'd transformed into a man any mother would be proud to claim, any woman would be thrilled to call her own.

Was change really possible for her? Could she go back to her life in Oklahoma City and welcome in new friendships and laughter? She didn't have to believe in love to open her heart up enough to allow a select few through.

She mentally shook her head. Once a tiger, always a tiger. A month spent on a ranch with special men bonded together by tragedy and trauma and among a small town full of people who obviously cared about each other couldn't turn her into something she was not. Sharing a meal, a kiss, and sex with Forest didn't change who she was at her core.

She knew in her heart she'd return to Oklahoma and resume the same dragon lady lifestyle she'd lived up to this point. She would be the same difficult taskmaster focused only on her job. Once a tiger, always a tiger. She wasn't sure why the thought depressed her just a little bit.

When the couple moved away, Forest stood and took her hand in his. "Things are starting to wind down and I want to be the last man to hold you tonight."

His words created a ball of warmth in the pit of her stomach. The song was slow and romantic, and once they hit the dance floor she moved into his arms and tried not to think about how much it felt as if she belonged there.

It was just a kiss. It had just been sex, and this was only a dance, and yet together she had to admit that they combined to fill her heart with a crazy feeling she'd never felt before.

She wanted to stop the dance immediately and she wanted the music to never end. She was conflicted as she'd never been before in her life, but ultimately she snuggled closer to the only man who had made her feel safe and cherished and beautiful.

He held her tight, one of her hands captured in his and pulled against his heart and the other arm wrapped tight around her back with his hand splayed as if in an attempt to cover every inch of her.

She would never forget this dance. She would never forget this man. He was burned into her brain with his sexiness, his kindness and how special he made her feel.

It was eleven-thirty when they finally got back into Forest's truck to head back to the ranch.

"It's a good thing we're leaving now," she said. "You know that at midnight Cinderella goes poof and turns back into the forensic anthropologist who needs to finish things up here."

"Then we'd better hurry back because I intend to get a Cinderella kiss before the anthropologist shows up again," he replied.

"And what makes you think I want a kiss?"

He grinned at her. "Oh, you want a kiss. You might not want to admit it, but that's another topic altogether."

She leaned back in the seat and stared out the passenger window where the darkness was broken only by an occasional light beaming out from a ranch house that dotted the landscape here and there.

She did want a kiss…his kiss. Darn him anyway. Not only did she want his kiss, she longed for it…had thought about it for most of the evening.

The only answer to her unusual desire was that she'd been submersed in "love" for the last several hours. She'd watched Lucas and Nicolette interact with each other, their eyes filled with the emotion she didn't believe existed, the emotion her father had taught her was false and something scientific facts couldn't prove.

She was in a love la-la land and she wouldn't manage to pull herself out of it until she was back in her room alone where she could get herself mentally into the real world, her world again.

By the time they reached the ranch and Forest parked the truck in front of her room, she'd shoved all thoughts out of her brain. The adrenaline that had filled her throughout the night was gone and exhaustion had taken over.

"You're tired," Forest said as they stood in front of her door.

She nodded. "I'm not used to kicking up my heels to a country Western band and socializing with the locals."

"You were a charming, dazzling date and I appreciate you agreeing to go with me." He stepped closer to her, so close her heart quickened despite her tiredness.

"Actually, I enjoyed myself. Everyone was so nice."

"I knew you would if you'd just let yourself." He looked at his wristwatch. "I have five minutes to get my Cinderella kiss." He took another step closer to her, and her heart leapt into her throat in sweet anticipation.

"Do you intend to take all of the five minutes?" she asked, surprised that her voice was half-breathy.

"I do, indeed." He leaned his head down to capture her lips with his. His mouth moved softly against hers, and without her volition her hands rose to rest on his upper arms as she pressed herself closer to him.

She couldn't help herself. The merest touch of his fired a desire through her that made her want to be as close as possible to him. He teased her lower lip with his tongue and she opened her mouth to allow him to deepen the kiss.

What had begun as tender and gentle quickly became

fiery and hot as their tongues battled and he wrapped his arms around her waist and pulled her tightly against him.

He was aroused, and she knew it would only take a single word from her and they'd be in her bed, naked and tangled together and satisfying each other.

She couldn't allow that to happen. It wouldn't be fair to either of them. As much as she wanted him, it wouldn't be right.

She halted the kiss and stepped away from him. She was far too vulnerable. Her brain had been taken out of her head and shaken around, leaving her confused about who she was and what she really wanted.

"Cinderella time is over," she said with a slight tremble in her voice. "It's time for the forensic anthropologist to get some sleep." She held out her hand for her room key.

His disappointment shone from his eyes as he dug her key out of his back pocket and handed it to her. She turned to unlock her door and was about to go inside when he called her name.

She turned back to face him. "Yes?"

"I just… I want you to know…never mind." He grimaced and then added, "I'll see you in the morning."

"Good night, Forest." She escaped into her room and locked the door behind her. She was afraid of what he'd been going to say to her. There had been such softness in his eyes and such fire in his kiss. She'd been afraid he was going to do something stupid like tell her that he was in love with her.

She didn't want to hear it. She didn't want to contemplate it. She couldn't be more wrong for him, and hopefully within a few more days she'd be gone and he could find the right woman to fulfill all of his dreams.

What she couldn't understand was why the thought of Forest being with the right woman created such a deep ache in her heart.

He'd almost told her last night. He placed the bridle on Twilight, pleased that the horse didn't fight him. He glanced toward the tent and grimaced. He'd almost told her he was in love with her last night, but at the last minute he'd changed his mind and chickened out.

It was late afternoon and she hadn't appeared in the tent entrance once during the day. She and Devon were obviously making progress.

He should be glad for them, but it was difficult to want a job finished when you knew that meant the end of time spent with the woman you loved.

But she doesn't believe in love, he reminded himself. And she probably wouldn't have appreciated his declaration the night before. It would have only made things awkward between them for the rest of the time she was here, and he didn't want that.

She would leave here and he would go back to loneliness and wishes unfulfilled. With his love for her in his heart, he couldn't imagine seeking another relationship with any other woman for a very long time to come.

Even knowing she would be leaving within the week, his heart, his head, his very soul was filled with her, and he didn't know how to stop himself from loving her.

Time. Time had healed much of the pain he'd experienced when his parents had died. Time was slowly working on the grief over Cass's death. It had simmered down from a sharp pang to a dull ache.

Weeks would pass, as would months and maybe eventually he'd forget he'd loved Patience so deeply. Maybe his heart would once again open enough to welcome love with another woman, a woman who shared his hopes and dreams for the future.

Dusty walked to the corral fence and set a boot on the lower rung. "Heck of a party last night," he said.

Forest left Twilight and walked over to join Dusty. "Yeah, it was a good time, though I couldn't help but notice that you never did ask Trisha to dance with you. She might have welcomed the invitation because I didn't see her dancing with anyone all night long."

"I know. Even drinking a couple of glasses of bubbly couldn't make me work up my nerve to approach her." Dusty heaved a deep sigh. "I've asked her out a couple of times, but she's always had an excuse to turn me down. Then she'll take a break and sit with me for a few minutes. Definitely mixed messages."

He took off his hat and raked a hand through his blond hair. "I swear, sometimes I feel like I'm still a scrawny kid again afraid of the world."

Forest laughed with a touch of sympathy. "There's nothing scrawny about you anymore, Dusty. You're a grown-ass man and maybe you should tell her exactly how you feel about her."

"It's not that I'm in love with her or anything that deep. I just want to get to know her better. All I really know is that she's a great waitress, she has a three-year-old kid and she lives at the motel. But I'm so attracted to her despite how little I know."

"Buck up, buttercup, and just go for it," Forest replied. "Even though you've asked her out, she probably doesn't know just how interested you are in her. Maybe she thinks you were just looking for a quick hookup. Or maybe she just thinks you like Daisy's Saturday night meat loaf and just ask her out because she's convenient."

Dusty raised his chin and gave a slow, thoughtful nod. "You're right. I need to let her know that I'm interested in her, and I'm not looking for a simple hookup. I need to make it clear to her that I'd like to get to know her better, away from the café and her job." A new determination shone from his eyes.

He lowered his chin and gazed toward the blue tent and then looked back at Forest. "So, you have all this great advice for me. Have you told the doc how you feel about her?"

Forest frowned. "What do you mean? She's just somebody I'm trying to keep safe."

Dusty eyed him knowingly. "You can spew that line to a lot of people, but I know you better than that. I see how you look at her and I watched you dance with her last night. You're crazy about her."

Forest took off his hat, raked a hand through his hair and then plopped his hat back on his head. "Okay, you're right. I'm in love with her, but telling her wouldn't make any difference. She doesn't believe in love or relationships. Besides, in the next couple of days she'll be finished with her work here and headed back to Oklahoma City."

"They don't have ranches around Oklahoma City?" Dusty asked innocently.

Forest looked at him in surprise. "Are you trying to get rid of me?"

Dusty tipped his hat back, his eyes glittering ice blue in the sunshine. "I'd like to work with you for the rest of my life. I owe you my life, Forest. But we both know you were never meant to spend the rest of your days living alone and working here. As much as I'd hate to see you go, I'd always want you to seek your happiness wherever it took you."

Forest looked toward the tent as emotion threatened to overcome him. "She could be my happiness, but it takes two and she isn't willing to change her beliefs to take a chance on me."

"That's a damn shame because as far as I'm concerned, nobody deserves a family and happiness as much as you."

Forest looked at Dusty with real affection. "You've been the little brother I never had and now this conversation is getting way too deep." He cleared his throat to swallow the emotions that had risen up inside him.

The conversation stayed with Forest long after Dusty had left the corral and he was once again working with Twilight. Would he be okay just to let Patience leave here without ever telling her what was in his heart?

If he spoke to her of his love for her he didn't expect her to suddenly reciprocate. Yet, each time he was with her the words of love pressed tight against his chest, leapt to the back of his throat as if begging to be spoken.

What could he possibly hope to gain by telling her?

Nothing, that's what he would get back from her. He focused again on Twilight. She was taking the bit well and it was time to move on to other equipment.

He might be known as a horse whisperer, but he definitely wasn't a woman whisperer. He didn't know how to change a woman's mind or how to make her love him.

It was almost four when Dillon's patrol car parked by the house. As the lawman made his way toward the tent, Forest could tell he wasn't happy. His stride was long and determined and he didn't acknowledge Forest's presence with a nod or a wave.

Uh-oh, it looked like more trouble. Dillon disappeared into the tent and a moment later he stepped back out, followed by Devon and Patience.

"How can I tell you how this happened when I don't know what happened?" Patience's strident voice rose in the air and pulled Forest out of the corral.

"First a missing skull and now this? Are you sure you haven't overlooked them?" Dillon asked.

"Don't question my work. Of course I haven't overlooked them," she replied, her voice louder and letting Forest know she was on the verge of one of her legendary full-blown explosions.

"What's going on?" Forest asked as he approached the three.

"What's going on is that Chief of Police Bowie is questioning my proficiency," Patience exclaimed, anger rife in her voice.

"Calm down before I pull you over my shoulders and dump you into the top of one of those corn silos," Forest retorted.

She stared at him in shock, and then to his surprise she laughed. "Okay, I deserved that. I was about to go completely ballistic."

"So, explain this to me again," Dillon said.

"We found all of the bones that would make up a palm, but we're missing the distal phalanges, the middle phalanges, the metacarpus…"

"Whoa," Forest interrupted her. "In plain English, please."

"The fingers. We're missing the fingers," she replied. "This particular skeleton has long finger bones, and none that are left in the pit are a match."

"More souvenirs?" Dillon asked to nobody in particular.

"That would be my guess," she replied, calmer now than she'd been before.

"If that's the case, whoever committed these crimes was a sick twist," Forest said in shock. It wasn't enough that these people had been murdered, but to discover that the killer had taken a skull and fingers from one of the victims made it even more heinous.

Dillon raced a hand through his hair, his features twisted in obvious disgust and frustration. "So what does this do to finishing up your work?"

"We've almost completed the fifth skeleton. The sixth should go relatively quickly and then the surprise seventh promises to be fast, especially if it all isn't there," Patience replied.

"Who would want to keep a skull and fingers from somebody they'd murdered?" Forest asked, still stunned by this latest bit of news.

"Somebody who wants to relive the crime over and over again," Devon said with a weary sigh. "Taking souvenirs from victims isn't exactly anything new."

"It's new for Bitterroot and the surrounding area. I can't wrap my head around what happened here so many years ago," Dillon said softly. "I just want to catch the person who did this. Whoever it is, there's no indication that he's been active since these crimes."

"Unless there's another pit of bones somewhere that hasn't been discovered," Patience said.

"That's a horrible thought." Forest's stomach turned at the idea of another pit of bones buried and yet to be discovered.

"Francine Rogers is supposed to be home sometime tomorrow. I'm hoping to talk to her and see if she remembers or has records of who she brought here to work for Cass," Dillon said. "I can't help but think because of the victims' ages, these were young men that Francine brought here to work on the ranch."

"Let's hope if Francine doesn't have records then she has an amazing memory," Forest replied.

"We've got to get back to work," Patience said. She looked at her wristwatch. "I still have an hour or so before my protective bodyguard shows up and forces me to stop working for the day." She shot Forest an affectionate smile.

"That would be me," Forest said agreeably.

"I'm out of here. Come on, Devon." She turned on her heels and with Devon closely behind her, they disappeared back into the tent.

"Thanks for your intervention," Dillon said to Forest

as the two men walked away from the tent. "I swear, I don't know why she was mad at me."

"She wasn't. She was frustrated and shocked by the new finding and she always takes those emotions and turns them into anger. You were there so she directed it at you."

Dillon shook his head. "I don't know, Forest. I just think she's an angry woman at heart."

"No," Forest countered. "Her heart is soft and sweet. She just doesn't access it very often. I think she's had to be tough for most of her life."

"At least she always calms down when you're around. All I know is that this is the crime scene from hell and I can only hope I never have to deal with something like this again for the rest of my life." Dillon's eyes were the color of cold steel.

"I swear to God if this killer is still around this area, I won't rest until he's behind bars. I've also contacted every law enforcement agency in the state to see if anyone else has dealt with anything like this."

"And has anyone?" Forest asked.

Dillon shook his head. "No, nothing like this mass grave of bones where the victims have been killed at different times. There have been crimes of mass murder in various counties across the state, but those have all been solved and the killers are in prison, and none of them involved a meat cleaver or a weapon like one."

"And still no word on who might have shot at Patience and me?"

"Raymond Humes insisted that he was having a meeting with his men at the time of the shooting and all of them were present. I've got Janis Little down at the Watering Hole listening to drunks' conversations and Daisy at the café doing the same, hoping that somebody will slip up and say something to indict themselves or somebody else. But so far nothing."

"I just wanted to make sure you weren't keeping a name from me to keep me from breaking a head," Forest replied.

Dillon smiled wearily. "I'd be more afraid of giving Patience a name and having her break a head."

Forest smiled at the idea of the warrior woman taking on anyone. Of course, Forest would never allow her to face any threatening man without him standing between them.

He and Dillon reached the corral, and after a bit of small talk, Dillon left. Forest remained outside of the corral. It was too late to continue working with the horse. Within less than an hour, he'd be pulling Patience out of the tent to clean up for supper.

It would be another evening of watching her interact with the cowboys and maybe sitting outside his room for a little meaningless conversation. She'd eventually retire to her room and he'd go to his with his heart already beginning to break because he knew it was mere days now and then she'd be gone forever.

Chapter 12

Patience sat next to Forest in the dining room and wondered vaguely when she'd gotten so comfortable here among all of the ranch hands, and with Forest.

Nothing and nobody else in her life had managed to distract her from her work, but Forest and his buddies always stole thoughts of her job away as she listened to them laugh and talk with both her and each other.

Tonight she needed to be distracted more than ever. The mystery of the missing fingers had been shocking. She'd worked lots of crime scenes in her short career, but nothing like this one.

The idea that the person responsible for such carnage might also be after her would have chilled her through and through if Forest wasn't at her side. She cast him a quick glance and smiled. Just looking at him made her feel happy and safe.

Happy. It was such an alien emotion for her. She was always satisfied when she finished with a crime scene. She was relatively content when reading her tabloids and munching on cheese puffs in the silence of her room. But she'd never experienced the kind of happy she'd found here.

"You wouldn't have really thrown me into the top of the corn silo, would you?" she now asked Forest, keeping her voice low enough that the others at the picnic table wouldn't hear her.

"Never," he replied and turned to look at her. "Being in a corn silo on the corn is dangerous. The corn swallows you up and you eventually suffocate. But if you'd continued heading in the direction of misplaced anger with Dillon, I wasn't averse to throwing you over my shoulder and taking you to one of the outbuildings and locking you up until you calmed down."

His eyes glittered with that teasing light that always created a pool of heat in the pit of her stomach. She loved the sound of his laughter, the quiet, often thoughtful talks they shared just before she retired for the night.

She was going to miss him desperately when she left here. She would miss that glimmer in his eyes and the fresh scent of him. She would miss his wonderful sense of humor and the way he managed to defuse her anger whenever she needed to be defused.

Most of all she would miss his soft touch, his heated kisses and the way he made her want to stop with her temper tantrums and learn to communicate her feelings better.

She hadn't told him yet that she and Devon could probably finish things up in the tent by tomorrow evening. She didn't want to admit to herself that she almost hated leaving here...leaving Forest.

"I heard you finished up with the sixth skeleton and are finishing up with the surprise seventh," Sawyer said, his copper-colored eyes gazing at her. "Any clues yet as to who might be the killer?"

"You'd have to ask Dillon about the investigation. I really shouldn't talk about any of my findings," she replied.

She wasn't trying to be secretive and she certainly hadn't unearthed any clues, but her own code of ethics didn't allow her to discuss her findings with anyone except the authorities. Besides, the grapevine around here seemed to know what was going on in the tent almost before it happened.

She could only hope that Devon shared that belief, especially when he was in town and dining or hanging out with the locals, including members of the Humes ranch.

The few Humes cowboys she'd met that night at the café had been uncouth and disrespectful. The men who surrounded her now were a different kind of animal, and like Forest, she found it difficult to believe that any of them could be guilty of the murders.

Although she couldn't know at this point for sure, she guessed that all of the seventh skeleton was there to be pieced together, leaving only the number-seven missing skull and number-five's missing fingers.

Dillon had his work cut out for him. It would be far too easy for this particular old crime to quickly become a cold case due to his inability to move any investigation forward.

Not my problem, she told herself. All she had to do tomorrow was complete the job of piecing together skeleton seven and then finish up with final notes. If and when Dillon managed to solve the crime, she'd already be long gone, probably working a new site and eating too many cheese puffs and entertaining herself by reading the tabloids.

Dinnertime ended as it always did, with many of them seated on sofas and listening to Mac McBride play his guitar and sing.

Patience found herself relaxing against Forest's side, warmed by his nearness and at peace with the familiar scent and contours of his body.

After several beautiful songs, Forest and Patience left the dining room. "Do you want to sit outside for a little while?" he asked when they reached the rooms.

"That sounds nice," she agreed, knowing that the end of her time here was quickly approaching.

He opened his room door and pulled out the two folding chairs they used whenever they sat outside. He unfolded them and they both sat beneath the pale light of the moon.

They were quiet for several minutes. Patience gazed up at the star-lit sky, listened to the night insects singing their songs and drew a deep breath of the distinctive scent of the ranch and the man seated next to her.

"You'll be leaving here soon." Forest broke the silence.

She looked at him, his features bathed in the moonlight. "I'm expecting to finish up with the last skeleton sometime tomorrow and then the next day I'll write up final reports for Dillon. Once that's done then we'll pull out and head back home."

"Then I guess I should take advantage of the time I have left with you."

She tensed. "What do you mean?"

"I mean there are still so many things I don't know about you, like what is your favorite color?" His voice was light and laid-back.

She wanted to ask him what difference it made, but instead she answered him. "That's easy. It's purple. What about you?"

"The blue of a clear Oklahoma sky," he replied. "Favorite food?"

"Two months ago I would have easily answered that it was cheese puffs, but now it's probably Cookie's barbecue beef or maybe the fried potatoes and onions he makes."

"We definitely agree on that one. I'd ask you what your favorite movie is, but I haven't been to a theater in years and I suspect you haven't, either."

"The only movie I remember going to was some kid movie when I was about five. My mother took me and cried through the whole thing. Even though I was young, I was mortified."

"She must have been a very unhappy woman."

Patience frowned and tried to think about the woman who had left her. "I guess," she finally replied. She'd never really thought about her mother being unhappy before.

"So tell me. What's the latest Hollywood gossip you've gotten from those tabloids you read?" he said in an obvious effort to change the topic of conversation.

"To be honest, I haven't read one for a couple of days now." She looked at him once again and then turned away. This was the strangest conversation they'd ever shared. Although on the surface his tone seemed light, she sensed a simmering tension beneath the pleasant tone.

She wanted to ask him what he was doing, but she didn't want the conversation to go any deeper. She was afraid of what he might say.

"I should probably head inside and get a good night's sleep," she said. She rose from the chair and pulled out her room key.

"But it's still early," he protested.

"I know, but I'd like to get an earlier start than usual in the morning."

Forest also stood. "Then I guess I'll be ready whenever you are." He hesitated a moment. "Good night, Patience," he finally said.

"'Night, Forest," she replied and entered her room. She changed into her nightgown and got into bed with a tabloid to read before going to sleep.

She flipped through several pages but found herself unengaged by the words and the pictures. Instead her head was filled with thoughts of everyone she had met and interacted with here on the ranch, people who obviously had a depth of caring for each other.

It had been like stepping on to an alien planet, so different from her isolation and cold environment of science. She closed the tabloid, shoved it back under the bed and then turned out the overhead light and got back into bed.

Her head filled with a vision of Forest. Yes, she was going to miss him when she returned to her own life. But they were never meant to be together. The best thing she could do for him was get out of here so he could find the woman who believed in love and family and happily-ever-after.

Cassie sat on the end of her mattress and stared at the wall opposite her bed, a small niggle of guilt wiggling through her. When she had first arrived at the ranch, the wall had held twelve pictures, each one of Cass with a different one of her young "cowboys."

Her aunt's face had radiated pride and love in each of the twelve photos, and it was telling that those pictures would be the first thing Cass would see when she awoke each morning.

Now those photos were stored away in a box on the top shelf of the closet hidden by dozens of shoe boxes of high heels she'd foolishly packed to come here. Instead the wall held an array of watercolors and oil paintings that Cassie had completed while she'd been here.

The images now on the wall were of the city she longed for, neon signs shimmering in a rain storm, a busy street of shoppers and a skyscraper with the morning sun beaming off glass windows.

If she closed her eyes, she could feel the heat from the sidewalks, smell the exhaust of buses and hear the honking of impatient taxi drivers.

Her store had sold clothing Nicolette found at discount rates by no-name designers and also original artwork painted by Cassie. Nicolette had since bought out her part of the business from Cassie, allowing her to pay the rent and utilities on the storefront for a couple more months.

After those months were up, Cassie had no idea what she'd do to keep the store open if she didn't sell the ranch by then. She was sitting on a gold mine. Raymond Humes had already contacted her to let her know if and when she decided to sell out, he wanted the first opportunity to buy the place.

Cassie knew her Aunt Cass would roll over in her grave if she sold the ranch to the silver-haired vulture next door, but Cassie had to think about maintaining her store. At the moment she was land-wealthy and relatively cash-poor, and rent wasn't cheap in New York.

She not only had to worry about rent and utilities at the store, but also on the apartment she hadn't given up when she'd come to Oklahoma.

She'd taken down the photos of her aunt with all the cowboys because each morning when she'd awakened and looked at them, they represented the past. The array of paintings that now greeted her each morning was the hope of a return to the future she'd always dreamed of for herself.

When she got back to New York City, her plan was to turn the entire storefront into an art gallery that would showcase not only her own work but also some of the street artists she found talented and undiscovered. She would make a success of it and prove all of the naysayers wrong.

She knew she was talented, and when she got back to the city she would work especially hard to assure her success. At least spending time on the ranch had given her a new work ethic.

All she had to do was get the crime scene gone from the property. Once Dillon released the land, she could put it up for sale and get back to where she belonged.

She didn't want to think about the men who worked here and what might happen to them when the ranch sold. It felt like breaking up a family, but she reminded herself that they were all grown men and perfectly capable of taking care of themselves. Ultimately she wasn't responsible for them.

She turned on the lamp on the nightstand and then went into the adjoining bath and got ready for bed. It was still relatively early, but she'd grown accustomed to ranch hours, which meant getting up with the sun and going to bed before ten.

Besides, the night before she'd begun to read the earliest of the diaries she'd found in the outbuilding written by her Aunt Cass.

To her surprise the diary was the thoughts of the young town girl Cass had once been when she'd first met her future husband, handsome rancher Hank Holiday.

Cassie was actually enjoying reading the musings

of a young woman falling in love and determined to get her man. Even though she knew the sad ending of Hank's death from cancer and Cassie's being killed in a tornado, she was surprised to discover that she liked reading about the journey the two had taken together.

When she sold the ranch, she'd dig out all of the other diaries that were in the outbuilding and have them shipped to New York. Nobody else would care about them but her and she felt a closeness with her aunt that she'd never felt from her own parents.

She climbed back into bed and picked up the old, yellow-paged book from the nightstand. Although Cass had left the ranch to Cassie, Cassie hadn't known her aunt very well.

She might not be keeping the ranch alive, but she could keep Cass alive by reading her story and maybe someday passing it on to children of her own.

She must have dozed off, for somehow she knew she was dreaming, and in her dreams she was standing next to each of the cowboys on the ranch while their pictures were taken together.

Cass stood nearby, smiling her approval, her blue eyes filled with affection as she looked at each of the "boys" she'd taken on and loved.

The scene shifted and Cassie was pounding a for-sale sign into the grassy area near the road in front of the property. Cass stood nearby, her eyes blazing in anger as she wielded her infamous bullwhip and hit the sign, taking it down to the ground.

Cassie came awake and sat straight up in bed, her

heart pounding. She drew in a deep breath and waited for the last vestige of the dream to leave her.

She wasn't sure what worried her more: the idea that somebody working on the ranch might be a killer, or selling the ranch and possibly being visited nightly for the rest of her life by the very angry ghost of Cass.

Chapter 13

It was just after noon when Devon left the tent and disappeared into the nearby big white van. Forest carried a sack lunch toward the tent. He assumed Patience had dismissed Devon for the lunch hour and it had been habit for Forest to provide Patience with a sandwich.

"Lunch time," he called from the tent entrance. He peeked a head in, not seeing Patience seated on her usual chair for the noon hour.

"You can come on in." Her voice drifted from the left of him, and he stepped in to see her leaned over the bone pit. He tried not to notice how cute her butt looked in the denim shorts.

She straightened up and blew upward to move a strand of her hair from her forehead. "It's almost done.

There's just a few bones left. I told Devon to go inside and start packing up the equipment."

"Then you should be feeling pretty good." He spoke around the lump that had risen in his throat at her words.

"I'm definitely feeling hungry." She took the bag from him. "Thanks." She sat on her chair and to his surprise gestured him to a nearby chair. She used a sanitary wipe to clean her hands and then opened up the bag and pulled out the sandwich.

She took a bite and chased it with a sip of one of her sodas. "I'm going to miss Cookie's sandwiches," she said. "He makes the best."

What about me? Are you going to miss me? He asked the questions only in his mind. "It's going to be strange not to have the tent on the property anymore," he said. "You managed to get the last two skeletons together pretty fast."

She nodded. "One of them was considerably larger than the other and that made it easier. The taller one is the one missing the skull and number five was the one missing fingers." She looked over at the two steel gurneys that held the last two remains. "I've only got a few more bones to finish number seven and they're still in the pit."

"Then no more missing bones?"

"Just the skull and the fingers of the one hand on the other skeleton, that seems to be all that is missing." She took another bite and chewed slowly, as if in deep thought.

She drank another sip of her soda and gazed at Forest. "I've worked a lot of scenes in my career, but this one is going to haunt me for a long time."

She had no idea how long she would haunt him after she was gone. But he'd decided to keep his feelings to himself, that there was no point in speaking of love and the dreams he wished for them together.

He cared enough about her to allow her to walk away unencumbered by his love for her. Why burden her with his desire for things that could never be…at least not with her.

"I only hope Dillon is able to find out something from Francine Rogers. I heard she's supposed to drive out and meet him at the police station in Bitterroot sometime tomorrow," he said.

"I'm not sure that identifying these victims will tell him much about the killer after all these years, but at least if he can identify them he might be able to provide some closure to their families," she replied.

Forest frowned. "A sad closure. I imagine most of the families of the victims either didn't care about what happened to them, or have wondered all these years if they were alive or dead."

"I know you don't have anyone wondering about you, but what about all the other men here? Do they have families someplace who might care? People who have been looking for them all of these years?" she asked and then popped the last bite of her sandwich into her mouth.

"It's hard to tell. I know in most cases, the men ran away from home or were thrown away by uncaring parents. From what I know, none of the men used an alias when they arrived here. Even though we're an hour and a half away from Oklahoma City, I imagine if somebody looked hard enough they would have been able to find their son. I don't know any of the men who have attempted to reconnect with family."

"What about Dusty? He was so young when he went out on the streets." She wadded up the paper bag and tossed it into a nearby trash bin.

"When I first met Dusty he had bruises on his face and arms. He complained of an earache and I suspected he had a ruptured eardrum. I thought the injuries had come from other street kids, but he'd been beaten by his father and apparently it had been happening from the time he was a toddler. He finally ran away, deciding life on the streets among strangers was better than getting beaten on a regular basis by somebody who was supposed to love him. I doubt that his father cared that he was gone."

"What about his mother?" she asked.

"I don't know anything about her. That's the only topic that Dusty refuses to talk about with me or anyone else."

"You'd never know where he came from by his sunny disposition and easy smiles." She took another drink of her soda and then added the can to the trash.

"Cass worked hard to teach forgiveness. Dusty forgives his father, but he has no desire to reconnect with him. Dusty looks forward, not back. That's pretty much the way we all are here. The past is gone and can't be changed, but the future is what we choose it to be."

"Speaking of looking forward." She got up from her

chair and walked over to the pit. "Lunch was good, but I need to get back to work."

"Then I suppose I should get out of here." Forest rose and headed toward the tent entrance but paused as she called his name.

"Come here and see if you see what I think I'm seeing," she said. She was once again bent over with her head nearly inside the pit.

Curious, he moved over to stand next to her and peered into the deep, wide pit that now held only a couple of bones. "What am I looking at?" he asked.

"There, right at the edge of the fibula bone."

Forest had no idea what a fibula bone was, but he was capable of following her pointing finger. "It looks like something gold and small."

Patience jumped down in the pit and moved the bone aside and then used her fingers to dig at the hard earth until she had the object in her hand.

Forest helped her out of the pit, and she opened her hand to reveal the object. "A ring," he said, stating the obvious.

"A man's ring," she replied. "I need to call Dillon."

"I'll call him," Forest offered and then smiled at her. "He's used to getting bad news from you and this could actually be good news, right?"

She didn't reply. She returned to her chair and sat staring at the ring, obviously completely focused on the unexpected find.

Forest pulled out his cell phone and called Dillon. When the call was finished, he returned to the chair next to Patience and sat silently while she studied the ring carefully.

They didn't speak until Dillon arrived. "What now?" Dillon asked as he entered the tent.

Patience held the ring out on her palm toward Dillon. "It was at the bottom of the pit. It could belong to one of the first victims or…"

"It could belong to the killer," Forest interrupted her.

"And it's possible that's the reason somebody didn't want you to get to the bottom of the pit," Dillon replied. He took the ring from her and studied it closely. "Looks like it's real gold with an onyx stone."

Forest frowned. "The odds of some kid off the streets wearing an expensive gold ring like that are pretty minimal. Street kids wouldn't flaunt something of worth that could be stolen from them."

"Still, it is possible that it was worn by one of the victims," Patience replied. "And it's equally possible that when the killer dumped the first body the ring might have accidentally slipped off his finger and fallen into the pit with the victim."

"I need to get this into an evidence bag," Dillon said. He gave a hard look to first Patience and then to Forest. "I don't want this find mentioned to anyone—and I mean anyone. This might be the first real clue I have to work with, and I don't want anyone else to know about it. I'm meeting with Francine tomorrow and she might remember who possessed this ring, but she's the only person I want knowing about it."

"I won't say anything to anyone," Forest promised.

"Mum's the word with me, too," Patience replied.

"Besides, I intend to spend the rest of today and to-morrow morning working on final reports for you. We should be pulling out of here sometime around noon tomorrow unless something else comes up."

Forest doubted that anything else would come up. She had been thorough, and by noon the next day she would be packed up and gone.

He fought the wave of grief that tried to take hold of him. He'd tried so hard to prepare himself for telling her goodbye, but no matter when it happened, it would be one of the most difficult things he'd ever done.

Dillon left the tent and Patience pointed to the pit. "I've still got work to finish up. I'll see you at five." She moved toward the pit and Forest left the tent.

He went back to the corral and began to work with Twilight. Within a month or two she'd be a great riding horse. Although all of the cowboys had their own mounts, Cassie didn't.

Twilight would make a perfect horse for her by the time Forest finished up the training. He had to let Cassie know that she needed to start working with the horse soon, so the two would bond and be perfect for each other.

At least it would be a project that might take his mind off Patience's absence, although he doubted that anything could do that.

After dinner that evening, Patience agreed to sit outside with Forest before going to her room. This was their last night together, he thought as they settled into their chairs in the waning twilight.

They sat silently, and as always he wondered what

she was thinking. Whether she knew it or not, she'd changed during her time on the ranch.

She'd softened, her temper appearing less often than it had initially. She'd allowed herself times of relaxation and laughter. She'd asked questions about the other men on the ranch, showing a curiosity about others that was incongruent to a loner.

Yes, she'd changed in so many ways except how he wanted her to change most of all. She hadn't transformed enough to want to share his dreams and his future. She still refused to discuss or even believe in love and any meaningful relationships.

"Beautiful night," he finally said to break the silence.

"It's a lovers' sunset," she replied and pointed to the west where the sinking sun cast vivid shades of pink and gold across the sky.

"Yes, it is," he replied, his heart aching as he remembered the kiss they'd shared with a colorful sunset painting the dusk.

He wouldn't attempt a kiss tonight. Kissing her again would hurt too much.

"Do you have another job waiting for you when you get back to Oklahoma City?" he asked.

"Not at the moment, but I'm sure it won't be long and I'll be called out for another job. In September I start lecturing at the college again."

"Do you enjoy interacting with the students?"

She turned to look at him. "I really don't have much interaction. I stand at a lectern in a huge auditorium and don't work closely with any of the students."

"What happens when you're called to a job?"

"I have a good assistant who takes over for me with the classes," she replied.

He raised an eyebrow. "You actually trust somebody else to do your job for you?"

"I make sure I have lectures ready and a thorough syllabus for the students. I don't mind turning that job over to an assistant. It's my work for law enforcement and with bones that I won't turn over to anyone else."

He gazed at her, her features clear in the rising moonlight. "Do you have any idea how deeply I'm in love with you?" The words slipped out of his mouth unbidden and there was no way he could take them back.

Patience stared at him, stunned by his words and momentarily speechless. She'd been so afraid that they were getting too close and certainly she had allowed him into her heart deeper than any other person in her life. But love? She had no space for that in her heart.

"Forest, I'm leaving tomorrow and you have your life here and I have my own in Oklahoma City. Besides, I know you want me physically. I also know you have this fanciful dream of a happily-ever-after and for some reason you've plugged me in to that picture."

His eyes narrowed and gleamed in the waning light of day. "I haven't 'plugged' you in to anything. Believe it or not, there have been plenty of women before you, women who would have been happy to share my fanciful dream. But I didn't love them the way I do you. I didn't want them to be my future. You're the woman I love with all my heart."

His words, along with his intense gaze, trembled inside her. How could she buy into what he was attempting to sell when she didn't believe the product existed? How could she make him understand that she wasn't meant for anything he wanted as he moved forward with his life?

"I have a career in Oklahoma City," she replied and felt a desperation she didn't understand.

"And I can pick up and buy a ranch there. I've got money saved up to make a move and I'd do it in the blink of an eye if it meant we'd be together."

"You'd really do that?" she asked. "You'd leave all of the men here, all of the relationships you've built over the years?"

"In a heartbeat if it meant being with you," he replied without hesitation.

She shook her head. "It doesn't matter, it's a moot point. You know I don't believe in love or happily-ever-after. I will never forget how good you've been to me, Forest. I'll never be able to thank you enough for protecting me, but somehow you've mixed up our closeness into believing that you love me."

He leaned toward her, his eyes glittering a sharp silver blue. "I don't *believe* I'm in love with you. I know I'm in love with you, and I think if you search your heart and shove away whatever fear is inside there, you'll realize that you love me, too."

"I don't have any fear," she protested. "I just know what I know and that is that love is a false premise based on nothing factual."

"Damn your facts. Damn the shell that encases your heart and keeps you from feeling," he exclaimed.

She sat back in her chair, as if pushed back by the force of his words and the tinge of anger that had deepened them. "I don't have a shell around my heart." Her face burned with the flush of an impending anger of her own. "Besides, the heart is just a muscle that pumps blood, it's not a place where love resides."

"You're right." His flat agreement surprised her, but he continued. "We all think of love being a function of the heart, but it actually lives in our brains. It's built on shared memories and unique connections. It is hormones and chemicals and all the things you talk about, but it's so much more than that."

"It's a fool's notion," she retorted. "And I don't like this conversation."

"I didn't figure you would because it's about feelings and emotions that are so different from the anger you use as a shield."

She shook her head vehemently. "Love doesn't exist and that's that."

"Did you learn that at your father's knee?" he asked.

Anger rose hotter inside her. "My father is a brilliant man."

"Maybe as far as book learning, but he obviously knows nothing about real life, about building dreams and loving another person so much you can't imagine your life without them."

Fear simmered inside her, the fear of long-held beliefs shattered, the fear of a vulnerability she'd never experienced before. "My father didn't want me to fall into the trap of believing in fantasies and fairy tales." She scooted her chair away from his, allowing her anger to relieve the alien emotions that had momentarily gripped her.

"You can't love me because I don't like it. I won't allow it," she exclaimed.

He laughed dryly. "You can control a lot of things in your life, Patience, but you can't control me and how I feel about you. I love you with all my heart and soul. You are the woman I want to wake up and see first thing in the morning and you're the woman I want to hold in my arms through each night. You are the woman I want to carry my children and share with me a future filled with family and ever-lasting happiness. You can't change my mind and you not liking it won't change it, either."

"I'm leaving tomorrow and I told you once, I warned you that when I left I wouldn't look back."

"I don't want you to look back," he countered. "I want you to look forward. I want you to search your soul. I know you love me, Patience, and I know it scares you. But it's nothing to be afraid of. Just embrace it, Patience."

She jumped out of her chair. She didn't want to hear anymore, she didn't want to see him anymore. Escape. More than anything she needed to escape as quickly as possible.

"I'm done here," she said and pulled her room key from her pocket.

"Of course you are," he said with a touch of bitterness. "Run...escape...that's what you do when you are feeling something besides anger."

She yanked her room key from her back pocket. "I'm

not running. We just obviously don't agree and I don't want to talk about it anymore."

"I just want you to think about one thing," he said as she headed for her door.

She paused and looked at him warily. "What?"

"If your father didn't believe in love, then why did he marry your mother?"

She stared at him wordlessly and then went into her room and slammed and locked the door behind her. She refused to think about the conversation that had just taken place.

She headed for the shower, needing a distraction. But even standing under the warm water for almost twenty minutes couldn't dissolve his words from her mind.

Why had he told her what he felt for her? Why had he scrambled her brain with talk of love and children and a future with him? She'd made it crystal-clear to him from the very beginning that she didn't do love, that she didn't believe in binding her life with anyone. Why hadn't he just kept his feelings to himself?

She'd always been perfectly satisfied in her isolation, with her work as her lover and partner. Her time here at the ranch, her time shared with Forest hadn't changed that.

Finally she stepped out of the shower, dried off and pulled on her purple nightgown and a pair of clean panties. She got into bed and pulled out a tabloid and a new package of cheese puffs, determined not to think about what had just occurred outside with Forest.

The tabloids were filled with news of breakups and

hookups, of new "love" and divorce proceedings. Why had her father married her mother?

The question popped unbidden into her consciousness, and she forcefully shoved it away. She didn't want to think. She refused to feel. By tomorrow night she'd be back in her own bed in her apartment and life would continue as it had before she'd come to this special ranch and the special people of Bitterroot and the Holiday Ranch.

A hollow wind blew through her, and she stubbornly refocused her attention on the slick magazine detailing the life of people she'd never know, people she had no desire to meet.

This was safe. This was her life, and the idea of opening herself up to Forest terrified her. How could he love her? Her own mother had walked away from her. Her father had only tolerated her. She was a shrew and the dragon lady, a difficult taskmaster and distinctly unlovable.

Yet she couldn't discount the utter conviction that had been in Forest's voice as he'd spoken of his love for her. She couldn't forget the softness of his gaze whenever it lingered on her.

Was it possible he found something about her to love? Was it possible karma or fate or whatever had brought them to each other for a reason? She flipped a page in irritation. She didn't believe in karma or fate. You just lived one day to the next without any grand plan in place.

Why did her father marry her mother? Patience closed the tabloid, rolled over on her back and closed her eyes. Why, indeed? She reached back to access memories she'd spent most of her years attempting to forget.

A vision of the two-story house where she'd grown up presented itself, along with a vision of her mother, Paula. She'd had red hair, too. She'd had long flowing locks that fell beyond her shoulders and emphasized delicate features and big green eyes.

She'd been an excellent cook, a good housekeeper and talented as an artist. One of Patience's very first memories was of her mother and her seated at the kitchen table drawing and coloring pictures together.

Then her father had entered the kitchen and berated them both for wasting time on such nonsense. Her mother's laughter had instantly transformed to tears and she'd gotten up from the table and stomped up the stairs to the master bedroom. Funny, she'd forgotten that particular memory until now.

The wall up the stairs to the second floor had been lined with framed photos. Patience frowned as she tried to bring those pictures to life in her head.

Her parents standing on the balcony of a cruise ship, both of them smiling and looking achingly young. Another image was of them standing in front of the house, her father gazing at his mother with a softness Patience had never seen before on his face.

Finally, Patience remembered their wedding photo. There was no question that they gazed at each other with a love that leapt out of the photo.

Love. Her father had married her mother because he'd been in love with her. Patience's heart stopped in her chest as the realization took full possession of her.

The man who had taught her not to believe in love had loved.

Why else would he have married? He'd been a self-sufficient man who didn't need a wife. He certainly hadn't shown any enjoyment in having a child. There had been no reason for him to get married other than for love.

She had no idea what dynamics had been at work that had ultimately forced her mother to leave, but she could only wonder now if bitterness had been her teacher.

After her mother had left her father, had he become so bitter that he was determined his daughter would never be hurt but also would never experience the joy of love?

Her heart began to beat again, faster, more frantic as the past faded away and thoughts of Forest bloomed in her mind. Forest, with his charming smile and teasing laughter, she'd been drawn to him from the moment he'd introduced himself to her.

He'd protected her from danger, putting his own life on the line for her. He'd forced her out of her comfort zone and into a new place that had become just as comfortable.

The fear that had always clutched her when she thought of loving somebody melted away as she remembered their sweet kiss by the silo and the picnic he'd planned just for her.

He'd forced her to be sociable with the others on the ranch. His smile made her smile no matter what was going on. Making love with him had been something she wanted to do again and again for the rest of her life.

Most importantly, he made her want to be a better woman, a better person. She'd been so afraid of everything he was offering her, and now she realized she didn't have to be afraid anymore.

Love.

It burst forth in her heart, it filled her soul and she wanted his dreams to be her own. She wanted to tell him right now, this minute, that she was in love with him.

She'd fought against it and tried to deny it, but there was no question that she was in love with Forest Stevens. She understood now why he had spoken of his emotions to her. When you realized you were in love, you wanted to tell the person as soon as possible. You wanted to start your life with them immediately.

But a glance at her clock let her know it was nearly one in the morning. He'd be asleep by now, and despite everything that simmered inside her, she didn't want to awaken him. Letting him know the depth of her love for him would have to wait until morning.

She turned off her light and got back into bed, still filled with the awe of the love she'd finally embraced. She'd clung to her father's beliefs for so long, she had become just like him, emotionless and cold.

She didn't want to be that person anymore. More important, she wasn't that person. It was time for the tiger to transform into something better, and she was more than ready for that. She wanted to be the woman Forest deserved. She wanted to take his love and give it back to him.

She was almost asleep when she heard a soft knock on her door. Forest! It could only be him. Maybe he had decided to give one more try at convincing her to look inside herself and discover the love she felt for him.

Wasn't he going to be surprised to find out that's exactly what she'd done. Eagerly she jumped out of bed and without turning on the light she unlocked and opened her door.

Surprise riveted through her, but before she could say anything a needle plunged into her neck. She stumbled forward as she tried to raise a hand to remove the syringe.

Her hand never reached her neck. Dizziness was followed closely by the dark of sleep...of death.

Chapter 14

Forest sat in a chair outside his room, waiting for Patience to make her morning appearance. It was almost eight and he was surprised she hadn't come out of her room yet.

He'd assumed she'd want to get an early start on finishing up her reports and getting out of here, especially after the conversation they'd had the night before.

He'd sworn he wasn't going to tell her that he loved her, but he hadn't been in control of his emotions, knowing that he had only one night left with her. And she'd reacted just as he'd expected her to, with a touch of horror and with a defensiveness he'd been unable to breach.

Maybe he'd been wrong about her all along. Maybe she really didn't love him. Although he could have sworn he'd seen love shining from her eyes, felt it radiating from her whenever they touched, whenever they were near.

It was possible she just saw him as a nice, big cowboy who had been her bodyguard during a difficult time on a job site and nothing more. It didn't matter now. He'd told her how he felt about her and she'd blown him off.

It was over. It was done, and this afternoon she'd be gone, leaving his dreams of a family and of a future in shatters. He'd pick himself up, brush off the reddish brown Oklahoma dirt from his butt and get on with life. That was the only choice he had.

Maybe she was late leaving her room this morning because she was reluctant to face him after the heated discussion they'd had the night before. She could hide out for a while, but eventually the job would call her and she'd open her door.

He looked up as foreman Adam Benson approached where he sat. "Sounds like you'll be getting off guard duty after today," he said.

"That's the plan. I'll be back to my usual schedule tomorrow," Forest replied.

"I know the rest of the men will be glad to have you back among them."

"It's past time," Forest agreed.

"I heard Dillon was meeting with Francine Rogers sometime this afternoon. Hopefully, she can give him some names or answers about this whole mess."

"Hopefully." Forest thought about the ring Patience had found. Did it belong to one of the victims, or had the killer inadvertently dropped it when he'd stuffed the first body into the pit beneath the floorboards of the old shed?

"Dr. Forbes is getting a late start this morning," Adam observed and looked at his watch.

"Yeah, I'm just about to knock on her door and rouse her," Forest replied. "I figured I'd give it another few minutes and see if she makes an appearance on her own."

If she was putting off seeing him after last night's debacle, she didn't have to worry. He didn't intend to talk about his feelings for her again. He just wanted to see to it that she finished her work safely and then she'd be gone from any danger here…and from him.

He and Adam chatted about ranch business for a few minutes, and then Adam headed toward the main house and Forest checked his watch once again. It was almost eight-thirty, definitely late for her to get to work. The sun had been up for hours, and for the last week she'd wanted to be in the tent as soon as it was light outside.

He stood in front of her door and after a moment of hesitation, he knocked. There was no reply. "Patience," he yelled and then knocked again, this time harder.

No sound came from the room. He tried the door-knob, surprised when it turned easily in his grasp and the door opened. Her bed looked slept in, but the bath-room door was open and it was apparent she wasn't in the room.

Don't panic, he told himself. She probably got up extra early to avoid seeing him and was already at work in the tent. Still, his heart beat a little faster as he hurried from her room and toward the blue tent in the distance.

When he reached it, there was nobody inside. He still refused to allow himself to think that anything might be wrong. He stepped up to the door of the white behemoth that had served as headquarters and living space for Devon. He knocked on the door and after a moment Devon answered.

"Good morning," Devon said.

"Have you seen Patience this morning?" Forest asked.

Devon shook his head. "I haven't seen her since she kicked me out of the tent yesterday so that I could start packing things up in here and get ready to head out. I just assumed she was in the tent finishing up reports."

The panic that Forest had tried to tamp down now roared out of control. "She isn't in her room and she isn't in the tent. I don't know where she is." His voice held the faint ring of alarm.

Devon frowned. "Have you checked the cowboy dining room? Maybe she had Cookie whip her up a late breakfast before finishing her work. She's definitely been eating better for the last couple of weeks."

"Maybe," Forest replied. Without saying another word he took off at a half run back toward the cowboy motel and the dining room in the back.

Let her be there. Even though it would be uncharacteristic of her to want breakfast and especially to go to the dining room alone, he prayed that she would be there. He broke into a full run as he rounded her room and headed for the dining area in the back.

He was half out of breath by the time he whirled into the dining room...the very empty dining room. "Cookie," he yelled.

Cookie stepped out of the kitchen and wiped his hands on a towel. "Too late for breakfast, too early for lunch," he said.

"Have you seen Dr. Forbes this morning?" Forest asked.

"Nope, she never shows up for breakfast." Cookie frowned. "Is there a problem?"

"Yeah, there is. I can't find her. I can't find her anywhere." Forest turned on his heels and left the dining room, his heart pounding so hard it threatened to burst out of his chest.

Where could she be? In trouble...she was in trouble. He didn't need facts or evidence to support his gut instinct. She was in danger and they needed to find her immediately.

He ran for the main house. There was only one way he knew to get everyone's attention as quickly as possible. Full-blown panic pumped his legs as he rounded the house to the front porch where a large bell hung. He rang it, the peals sounding a loud frantic tone around the ranch.

Cassie flew out of the front door. "What's happening?" she asked, her eyes wide with concern.

"I can't find Patience. Have you seen her this morning?"

"No," Cassie replied. "What do you mean you can't find her?"

"She's not in her room, she's not in the tent and she isn't in the dining room. I can't find her anywhere."

By that time the cowboys began to arrive, some on foot and others on horseback. "What's going on?" Dusty asked worriedly. All of them knew that the bell was only rung in case of an emergency.

"I can't find Patience. You all need to spread out and check every outbuilding and every inch of the ranch," Forest replied, his panic deepening to a tone he scarcely recognized.

The men didn't wait for further instructions. They took off and disappeared from the front of the house.

"I'll call Dillon," Cassie said worriedly. "She's got to be here someplace. We'll find her, Forest." She disappeared back into the house.

Forest fought the instinct to fall to his knees as a sense of sheer horror swept through him. Her bed had appeared to have been slept in, but for how long? In all the times he'd entered her room when she was awake, the bed had always been neatly made up.

The unmade bed spoke of something bad. She normally didn't just get up and go directly to work. She made her bed. He mentally shook himself. He was obsessing about a bed when he should be doing something to find her. But still questions plagued him. Why would she have left her room by herself? And how long had she been missing?

It hadn't been that late when she'd angrily stormed off into her room. There was no way of knowing when exactly during the night or early morning hours that something had happened to her.

Action. He needed action to drive the horror of possibilities out of his mind. She wasn't a stupid woman. There was no way he believed she'd just decided to wander around the ranch without his protection.

Even though her job was pretty much finished here, she had to know that danger could possibly still find her. Besides, she wasn't one to alter her routine. If she wasn't in her room and she wasn't in the tent, he had no idea where else she could be.

All he knew was that he needed to join the others in the search. He raced from the porch to the stables where he saddled up Thunder in record time. He could cover more ground on horseback than on foot.

There was little relief to see the others searching a variety of places. There would be no relief until she was found safe and sound. Thunder's hooves against the ground mimicked the frantic beat of his heart as he headed toward the barn.

Behind him he heard various men yelling updates. "Utility shed is clear," Dusty's voice rang out.

"She's not in the garage," Brody shouted.

"Dr. Forbes."

"Patience!"

Everyone called her name, and building after building was checked with no success. With every minute that passed, Forest felt as if his heart ripped out of his chest.

Where was she? What could have happened to her? Who would want to harm her at this point in the investigation? She'd been done except for writing a few reports. She shouldn't have been a threat anymore to anyone.

Was this about the ring she'd found? But nobody knew about it, so what could that have to do with anything? With her disappearance?

A modicum of relief swept through him as Dillon pulled in with three patrol cars behind him. The more men, the more thorough the search, and there was still so much ground to cover. Forest rode up to the side of Dillon's car.

"Is she still missing?" Dillon asked through his open driver window.

Forest gave a curt nod, momentarily unable to speak around the huge lump in the back of his throat. He moved Thunder away from the side of the vehicle, and Dillon got out and motioned for the men in the other cars to do the same.

"Spread out," he instructed his men. "We're looking for a small red-haired woman."

Forest told himself that the more people searching, the better the odds that she was found, but he couldn't halt the sickness in his gut, a sickness that was born from the fear that they would never find her, or if they did, it would already be too late.

Sunshine on her face. It warmed her skin like Forest's kisses warmed her heart. A tiny headache danced across her forehead, and she opened her eyes to find herself staring directly at the morning sun.

Her brain worked to make sense of the fact that she was peering up through a large opening surrounded by metal. Her bedroom didn't have any metal in the ceiling. She certainly couldn't see the sun inside her room when she was on her back in bed.

She wasn't in her bed!

She slammed her eyelids closed. A dream. Surely

she was dreaming. Yet the sun felt so hot, and despite the fact that her eyes were closed, she saw its brilliance through her eyelids. She wasn't sleeping and this wasn't a nightmare.

Kernels of corn. She was on top of them. Her heart jumped a dozen beats and she opened her eyes once again. She was in a corn silo. She didn't move, was afraid even to breathe.

She wasn't completely flat on her back, as her legs were slanted outward and buried to just under her knees in the yellow corn. Dust swirled in the air, tickling at the back of her throat, but she didn't dare sneeze or cough.

How had this happened? Still scarcely breathing yet with her heart pounding so fast she was half-breathless, she tried to remember how she had gotten here and who had put her in here.

The last thing she remembered was that she'd been in bed, thinking about Forest, excited for morning to come so that she could tell him that she was in love with him. She'd had no idea how their future together would work, but she had been confident that they would figure things out, that they would make it work no matter what the obstacles.

They were going to get married and have children and pot roast Sundays whenever she wasn't on a job and working on the weekends. He'd work on their ranch and she'd be his life partner and they would live happily ever after.

The sunlight blurred as tears sprang to her eyes. So, what had happened between then and now? She'd almost been asleep, eager for the morning to come so that she could tell Forest of her love for him. There had been a knock on the door.

She frowned. Who had been at the door? A sting in her neck…a wave of dizziness and then nothing. Who had done this to her and why? Who had attacked her in the middle of the night and brought her here to die?

By this afternoon she would have been leaving the ranch. Her part of the investigation would have been over. Why attack her now?

Her legs twitched with nerves, and to her horror they sank deeper down into the corn, now burying her to a mere inch below her knees. In that instant she recognized the true danger she was in, that unless somebody found her soon, the corn would drag her down into its deepest depths and suffocate her.

It was possible nobody would find her until the silo was emptied out and then all they'd find would be her dead body. She was even afraid to scream. By drawing in enough air to produce a good scream she feared she'd displace more corn and be buried deeper.

There was a steel ladder descending into the silo, but it was too far away for her to reach and there was no way she could swim through the corn to grab it. Any chance at all of surviving depended on her staying perfectly still.

She gazed up at the sun once again. It was rising higher in the sky with each moment that passed. Surely it was late enough that somebody would know she was missing by now.

The cowboys were all probably out looking for her. But who would think to look inside the top of a corn silo? Whoever had done this to her had assured her death.

Who? Who had done this and why didn't she remember?

She fought to find some modicum of hope. It wasn't fair. It wasn't the way things were supposed to end. She'd finally realized the depth of her love for Forest. She'd embraced his dreams as her own.

It just wasn't fair that now she wouldn't get a chance to act on her love, to build that future that promised bliss.

She wasn't supposed to die by being smothered in a vegetable she rarely ate. But it appeared that it was going to happen. She would suffer a slow, torturous demise as she sank deeper and deeper into the corn.

Even though she didn't want him, even though she'd pulled out all of her defenses the night before, Forest was frantic as another hour passed and still there was no sign of Patience anywhere on the property.

Even Devon had left the cool of the trailer to help in the search, his white lab coat like a beacon against the pasture as he walked from one building to another.

Dillon's men were also on foot, while the rest of the cowboys had taken to their horses to hunt for the missing woman. Forest and Dillon stood in Patience's room, hoping to find an answer as to what had happened to her by being in the place Forest had last seen her enter.

"It's obvious she went to bed," Forest said. His heart ached when he saw the edge of a tabloid peeking out from under the bed. Had she been reading one of those when something terrible had happened? Had she escaped into her world of fantasy to negate Forest's words of love for her?

Dillon checked the door carefully. "Nothing appears to be tampered with and there's no sign of forced entry."

"It was unlocked when I opened it this morning." Forest looked around the room and then went into the bathroom and checked the clothing in her laundry bag. He then went back and looked in the chest of drawers and checked through the clothes it held.

"Wherever she is, I think she's in her nightgown. I don't see it anywhere here." He fought against the burn of tears in his eyes. "That means she was probably taken at some point in the middle of the night." Which meant she'd been missing potentially for eight hours or more.

"It's possible she isn't even on the property any longer," Dillon said, his gaze slightly sympathetic as he looked at Forest.

Forest fisted his hands at his sides. "Dammit, why didn't I hear anything? I'm a light sleeper. If there had been a struggle in here I should have heard something."

"If it's any consolation, it doesn't appear that a struggle took place," Dillon replied and looked around the room once again. "And that means she opened her door to somebody or she simply took off on her own. There's no sign in this room that a crime actually took place here."

"A crime definitely took place," Forest replied forcefully. His gut twisted into a dozen knots. "There's no way she would have just decided to get up in the middle of the night and leave in her nightgown to run away or take a midnight walk or whatever. She had reports to finish up for you and she's a professional. Only something bad happening to her could account for the fact that she isn't here and finishing up those reports."

"I think I'll take a couple of men and go talk to Raymond Humes and his men," Dillon said. "It's a long shot, but maybe one of them knows something about this."

Dillon left the room and Forest remounted Thunder. He knew Dillon would find no answers at the Humes ranch. He was beginning to believe they weren't going to find any answers on this ranch.

His brain was overloaded, his emotions nearly wrung dry as he headed aimlessly toward the pasture. Was she still someplace here on the ranch?

By now all of the outbuildings had been checked with no sign of her being in any of them. Without any success, the urgency that had marked the beginning of the search had eased somewhat as the sun rose higher and higher in the sky.

Although the other cowboys were still sweeping the ranch land, a sick hopelessness filled Forest's heart. He didn't know where else to look. He couldn't imagine where she might be, and he couldn't forget Dillon's words that she might not be on the property at all. Enough time had lapsed that she might be miles away from the ranch and the small town of Bitterroot.

A weary hopelessness blurred his vision with the mist of impending tears as he steered Thunder in the direction of the pond and the place where he and Patience had shared their picnic. She had to be here somewhere—he refused to believe that she'd been kidnapped and taken away.

In the back of his mind he hoped that he would discover her sitting in the grass beneath the leafy tree where they'd had their picnic. She'd be stretched out napping, unaware that anyone was worried about her.

She'd wake up and tell him she'd come here to say a final goodbye to the ranch and had accidentally fallen asleep. Even though she didn't love him, despite the fact she would never be a part of his future, he'd be all right just knowing she was safe and unharmed.

Of course when he reached the tree near the pond where they had shared their picnic, she wasn't there. He dismounted Thunder and walked to the wooden pier over the pond. He sank down to sit and tears began to flow.

He hadn't cried since the day of his parents' funeral, but now he couldn't stanch the deep sobs that racked through him.

Too late. She'd been gone too long. They'd checked everywhere they knew to look with no success. She was gone. He was supposed to protect her, to keep anything bad from happening to her, but he'd failed. He'd failed miserably.

There was no question in his mind that somehow she'd been taken from her room by somebody. She wouldn't have just left of her own volition in the middle of the night clad only in her nightgown. That didn't make sense, and Patience would never do anything that didn't make sense.

He not only couldn't figure out the who, but he also

couldn't guess at the why. She was finished here. The bones had all been retrieved and the skeletons put together and taken away.

Why take her now? What danger could she possibly threaten anyone with at this point in time? Again and again those questions played in his mind. He swiped angrily at his tears. Sitting here and allowing his emotions to rule was accomplishing nothing.

He pulled himself up from the pier, wondering what he should do next.

Chapter 15

Patience closed her eyes as the corn ate an inch more of her legs. It was like quicksand, slowly tormenting as it pulled at her in an attempt to swallow her whole.

As her legs sank, she fought the impulse to use her arms or her upper body to counter the sink. She was at a forty-five-degree angle, almost "standing" with her upper body still free.

But she knew it wouldn't be long before the corn would shift, or she would make an involuntary move that would suck her completely down under.

Part of her wondered why she was still mentally fighting what seemed like the inevitable. Why didn't she just allow the corn to have her in one fast movement instead of letting herself be swallowed inch by agonizing inch?

The instinct of survival was obviously greater inside her than the resignation of death—even a slow, suffocating death. She knew she was foolish, but she was waiting for some kind of a miracle.

Maybe if she focused enough she would be able to levitate up, or shift to the side where she could grab hold of the ladder rungs and pull herself to safety.

Perhaps her miracle would come in the shape of an oversized vulture swooping into the top of the silo and plucking her out, or a big, strong man…a man like Forest, who by some trick of magic found her.

It was funny, and she might have laughed at herself if she didn't know that in doing so she would descend deeper. She was looking for a miracle. She was a woman of science and facts, yet when staring at death, she desperately yearned for an unscientific miracle to happen.

She didn't give a damn about facts or scientific evidence. She wouldn't even ask any questions if a straw-stuffed scarecrow suddenly sprang to life and jumped into the corn to pick her up and carry her out and away from the silo.

The heat inside the structure had increased, stifling…sweltering. Her nightgown clung to her damply as she sweated and tried to keep breathing despite the dusty, suffocating hot air. And she was so thirsty. She longed for just a single sip of one of her cold sodas, or at the very least a tepid glass of water.

Of all the ways she thought she might die, drowning in a corn silo had not even been on her long list. There had certainly been times when she knew Devon would have loved to throttle her.

She suspected that there had been moments over the past month and a half that even Forest might have wanted to hang her from the nearest tree. Dillon had probably fought the impulse to put a bullet through her head to halt her haranguing of him, and then there were those nasty cowboys from the Humes ranch that she had ticked off.

It was shocking now thinking back over the past couple of years of her life and her work and realizing how many people she'd offended because of her quick temper, how many people might have wished her harm.

If only she could go back, get a do-over with the discoveries about real life, about good people and with the love that Forest had taught her burning in her heart. So many lessons learned and now no chance to be the person she most wanted to be.

A single sob escaped her, and she fought against the second that begged to be released as her legs sank a little bit deeper.

Who had put her here? Why couldn't she remember? It was like after the blow on the back of her head that had knocked her unconscious when the events leading up to the attack had been fogged in darkness.

All she remembered was her heart filling with love for Forest, a love she'd tried to deny and then a knock on her door.

Forest, his face filled her mind's eye. If she was going to die, then when she took her final last dying gasp, she wanted her final thought to be of him.

He'd made her rethink her life and the past as it had been told to her. As important as anything else he had done, he'd made her realize that it was possible her mother hadn't just walked away from them with the intention of abandoning her forever.

After she'd left, perhaps her mother had tried to see Patience; maybe she had even wanted custody. Patience had no idea what her father might have hidden from her in his silent bitterness. She'd been too young, and as she'd grown, she'd been fed stories that might or might not have any basis in truth. In any case, at this point, it didn't matter.

Forgiveness for her mother flooded through her as she once again closed her eyes against the bright sunshine. She could even find a modicum of forgiveness for her father in the depths of her heart. Whatever had happened between her parents had broken them both in ways Patience would never understand.

She certainly now understood how broken she had been before a big, protective and loving cowboy had stepped into her life.

Once again she filled her mind with a vision of Forest. A strange peace swept over her as the corn beneath her shifted and she waited for death.

Forest stared at the nearest corn silo. The single moment when he'd kissed Patience there had been the instant she'd completely captured his heart. He started to turn away, but paused as something unusual caught his eye.

There…on the fourth rung of the steel ladder that led up the side of the nearest silo, something white fluttered in the slight breeze. Curious, he walked over to the ladder to check it out.

It was a piece of white material torn from something and trapped by the head of a rusty screw. It hadn't been there the last time he and Patience had been here.

He plucked it off the screw. It was white, thick cotton, and as he held it in his fingers his gaze moved up to the top of the silo.

"No way," he muttered beneath his breath. Yet, he remembered the conversation he and Patience had shared, when she'd not only told him about her bad experience near a silo, but also her fear of them.

Had somebody been hiding nearby? Had somebody overheard that conversation and decided to put her in a place she feared most?

He shoved the piece of cloth in his pocket and grabbed the third rung and began to climb up the side of the tall structure. He told himself that he was a fool, that there was no way she could be inside the silo, yet his heart didn't get the message and began to bang against his ribs in a frantic rhythm.

He climbed faster and faster. If she had been dumped inside, by now it was probable that the corn had swallowed her whole and he'd never know for sure if she'd been there or not.

The instinct would be to attempt to "swim" to safety, a deadly choice that had killed many a ranch hand who had climbed down into a silo all over the country.

He was halfway up the ladder when Dusty appeared on his horse below. "Forest, what in the hell are you doing?" he yelled up.

Forest didn't slow his pace. "Checking out a crazy impulse," he replied, his feet and hands moving faster as he got closer to the top.

He heard no screams, no shouts for help, but if this was where she'd been put hours ago, then it was possible she was already gone, buried deep within the grain.

His grief had already been all consuming, but now it once again ripped at his guts and tore at his already tattered heart. He was vaguely aware of Dusty below as he reached the top of the silo.

He peered inside and a stunned gasp escaped him. "She's here!" he yelled down to Dusty. She was sprawled on her back, her arms stretched out on either side of her and her legs from the knees down buried in kernels of corn. Her eyes were closed.

"Patience!" His frantic voice echoed off the metal sides.

Her eyes snapped open and he nearly fell off the ladder as relief shivered through him. He'd thought she was dead, but her eyes simmered with terror.

"Don't try to talk and don't move." He threw a leg over the top and grabbed on to the ladder that was inside the silo. "I'm coming. You're going to be all right. I'm going to get you out of here." The words tumbled from him as he scrabbled down the ladder.

"I don't like this, Forest. I really don't like this." She barely breathed the words.

"I know, honey, and I'm going to get you out of here as quickly as possible." He reached the spot where the corn met the ladder. With one hand he clung to the ladder, and with the other he leaned out and stretched in an attempt to grab her hand.

So close, but still too far. Dammit, she was just inches from where he could reach her, but those inches might as well be a mile.

He grabbed his gun from the holster and shoved it in the back of his jeans waistband, then quickly tore off his belt, the holster falling to the top of the corn by the ladder.

He could have tried to lay his body flat upon the corn and attempt to reach her that way, but he couldn't be sure of how stable the grain was, and he would be of no help to her if he only managed to get himself sucked down to death with her.

He looped the belt and fastened it so that it was secured to the ladder. With one hand he held on to the belt buckle and propped his feet against the ladder so that he could swing himself out far enough to be able to grab her hand.

She didn't speak as she watched him get into position, but her terrified eyes told him all he needed to know. He leaned out and grabbed her hand, but her skin was slick with sweat and slipped out of his.

A sob escaped her. Forest didn't attempt to console her. He couldn't be moved by her horrified cry. His sole focus was to save her life. He wiped his hand on his jeans and reached out again, this time managing to grab her by the wrist.

He held tight, knowing it was going to take every ounce of his strength to pull her from the corn and toward the ladder. "Just lie still and let me do the work," he instructed tersely. If she tried to help him or to help herself in any way, she might only sink deeper, and he already had to pull her legs out from under the heavy corn.

A shadow from above momentarily distracted him. He glanced up and saw Dusty at the top. "We're getting plywood," he shouted down.

Forest didn't reply. Planks of plywood could be laid on top of the corn to aid in safety in a situation like this, but Forest had no intention of waiting for men to get planks into place. He needed to get her out of here right now.

Closing his eyes, he began to pull on her wrist, praying he could dislodge her and get her to the ladder without wounding her or breaking her tiny wrist bones.

It took all of the strength he possessed and he gasped in relief as she slid toward him just an inch. He'd moved tree limbs that weighed more than Patience. *You can do this*, he told himself. *You have to do this*.

She moved another inch closer, her legs slowly being pulled loose from the corn that sought to claim her. She released another sob, the sound welcome to him for it spoke of life.

Finally her legs came free and he slid her across the top of the corn and to the ladder. She grasped the rung with both hands as he perched his body just behind hers.

"Can you make it up the ladder on your own?" he asked.

She nodded and began a slow ascent upward. He quickly removed the belt that had given him the stretch that he'd needed to reach her. He grabbed it and his holster and then followed behind her.

Dusty remained at the top of the ladder and helped her over the top and to the other side to climb down. Even though she was safe, she was probably suffering from dehydration and exhaustion. She would need immediate medical attention.

And he needed answers. Who had done such a heinous thing? He certainly didn't believe she'd climbed up the silo on her own and somehow accidentally fallen inside. This had to be one of her worst nightmares.

When he reached the top, he looked down to see all of the men gathered at the silo's base, along with Devon and Dillon and his men. Cassie was there as well, her arms reaching out to embrace Patience as her feet touched the earth.

Forest raced down the ladder, where Patience had sunk to the ground in Cassie's arms, her face white in exhaustion. "She needs to get to the hospital," he said.

He fought the impulse to go to her, to pull her up and into his arms and feel her heart beating against his own. But he had no right, and in any case he wasn't what she needed. He stepped back from her and the others.

"How did this happen?" Dillon crouched down beside her. "How did you get into the corn silo?"

"I don't know... I just woke up and I was there." Her voice was thin and reedy and sweat still plastered her hair to her scalp and shone on every inch of her bare skin.

"Get her to the hospital," Forest said to Dillon. "You can question her on the way."

It took fifteen long minutes for Dillon to get her in his patrol car and pull away. Forest watched the car until it disappeared out of sight.

She would be okay. At the hospital she would get the necessary fluids that had been depleted from her body. They'd even feed her, and she wouldn't be released until the doctors were sure she was ready to be released. She wouldn't fight them, not after the trauma she had suffered through.

The other cowboys had dispersed to get back to work. Dillon's men had left, Devon had disappeared into the trailer and Cassie had returned to the house.

Forest found himself standing in front of his room, Dusty at his side. "Are you all right?" Dusty asked in concern.

"I will be once my adrenaline stops spiking," Forest replied.

"We've had some weird stuff happen in the last couple of months, but this definitely tops the list of everything else," Dusty said with a frown. "She said she just woke up in the corn, but she had to have gotten there somehow."

"I don't know if she was just too scared and confused to remember what happened or if she was somehow drugged and carried to the silo." The sickness that had filled his soul when he'd believed her dead slowly began to dissipate.

If he hadn't ridden out to the pond or if he hadn't gazed at the corn silo, she might have never been found alive. He remembered what had drawn him to the silo in the first place.

He reached into his front jeans pocket and pulled out the piece of white cloth that had captured his attention. He stared down at it and worked it with his fingers.

"What's that?" Dusty asked curiously.

"It was caught on a nail in one of the silo ladder rungs. It was what first made me think about checking the silo." Forest frowned. "It's too heavy to be part of a T-shirt."

"You think it was torn off the clothing of whoever dumped her in the silo?" Dusty asked. He stepped closer to eye the piece of material. "It doesn't look like anything any of us would wear."

"No. No, it doesn't." Forest stared toward the blue tent in the distance.

"What are you thinking?" Dusty asked.

"I'm thinking that we thought the attacks on Patience might have come from one of the Humes cowboys, and then we assumed it was the person who had killed the victims whose bones were in the pit. But maybe the person who wanted her dead was much closer to her than we thought."

Dusty looked at the tent and then back at the material. "Part of a lab coat?"

"Feels that way to me." Forest shoved the cloth back into his pocket and instead rested his hand on the butt of his gun, which was back in its holster around his waist.

"Maybe you should call Dillon," Dusty suggested, a hint of concern in his voice. "This is his job, Forest."

"You're probably right," Forest agreed, but a rage had begun to build inside him. "But Dillon is busy. He's taking care of Patience right now."

He walked toward the white trailer parked next to the blue tent and was aware of Dusty calling Dillon on his cell phone. But Forest was filled with a rage that wouldn't wait for Dillon to get back to the ranch.

Forest thought of the vision of Patience in the corn, of the terror that had darkened the hue of her beautiful eyes and the intense heat and dust that she had endured. Even if the corn hadn't eaten her alive, eventually she would have died from dehydration.

He walked faster to the trailer and once again touched the butt of his gun. He might just be willing to spend the rest of his life in prison to avenge what had happened to the woman he loved.

Chapter 16

Forest first went into the tent, where Patience's lab coat was slung over the chair in front of the computer. He picked it up and checked it for tears, trying not to notice the sweet scent of her that clung to the garment.

It appeared to be in perfect shape and so he hung it back on the chair and moved to the other white lab coat that was draped across the back of the chair where Devon normally sat.

He checked it inch by inch as his heart echoed in his ears with the beat of barely suppressed wrath. *You could be wrong*, he told himself when he found no tears in the coat.

He pulled the material from his pocket once again and held it between his fingers in one hand and grabbed the lab coat with the other. They felt the same in weight and texture.

There was no way Devon had only one lab coat with him. Their work was dirty and the tent was stifling and the two of them had been here working for well over a month. Besides, Forest knew that Patience had several with her because he'd seen her throw them in the washing machine.

He was sure that Devon had to have several more identical coats in the trailer, and his gut told him that one of them would have a tear that perfectly matched the scrap of cotton in Forest's hand.

He shoved the cloth back in his pocket and once again touched his gun. It would have been easy for Devon to follow Patience from the tent the night she'd been hit over the head. The man could have easily made his way back to the trailer in the darkness only to re-emerge when they'd found her on the ground uncon-scious.

Forest had no idea if Devon had a gun or not, but it would have also been simple for Devon to hide among the trees and try to shoot them and then meld into the ensuing fracas as a concerned bystander.

Nobody paid much attention to Devon's whereabouts. He was a respected scientist, Patient's assistant, and For-est assumed except for his trips into town for meals, he was always in the confines of the trailer.

But he could have been in the shadows of the night during the two attacks, and while Patience might not remember at this moment what had happened the night before, she certainly would have opened her door to her trusted assistant no matter what the time of night.

Forest mentally stacked up the circumstantial evidence against Devon and then left the tent. He banged on the trailer door at the same time he saw Dusty running toward him.

Devon opened the door and looked at Forest in surprise. "Forest, what's going on? Has something happened?"

Devon wore no lab coat at the moment. He was clad in a short-sleeved blue shirt and a pair of navy slacks. He was big enough, stout enough to carry an unconscious woman as small as Patience anywhere he wanted to take her.

"No, nothing has happened. I was just wondering if you'd step into the tent and answer some questions for me," Forest replied as he worked to keep his voice pleasant and nonthreatening.

Devon frowned. "Okay," he said slowly. He stepped down from the trailer and as he did Forest looked at Dusty. "Don't let him go anywhere." Dusty drew his gun and trained it on Devon.

"Hey...what are you..."

Devon's protest was quieted as Forest stepped up into the trailer and slammed the door behind him. The steering wheel and two seats were the only things normal about the behemoth recreational-like vehicle. Behind the seats each side was lined with stainless-steel counters holding equipment Forest had never seen before.

Beneath the counters were refrigerated spaces and above, built-in cabinets that held more equipment and bottles of liquids. At the very back of the vehicle was the private area where Devon stayed. There was a mini-fridge, a small microwave, a two-burner stove and a tiny bathroom with a shower.

Beneath the single bunk bed set high in the back was a clothes rack where slacks and shirts hung neatly on hangers along with three lab coats.

Forest yanked the first one off the hanger and went over it inch by inch, seeking a missing piece that would confirm his identification of the guilty person.

Finding nothing, he tossed the coat on the floor and pulled the second one from the hanger. His heart stopped as he spied the pocket with a jagged tear and an absent piece of cloth. He pulled the material he'd found at the silo out and matched it to what was missing on the pocket.

It fit. The jagged edges came together well enough for him to know that the errant piece of cloth that had been on the rung of the ladder up the silo had come from this particular lab coat.

He gripped the jacket tight in his fist, once again fighting against a killing rage. Devon Lewison, the man Patience had probably trusted the most, Devon, the assistant who had worked with her on dozens of jobs, had tried to kill her. He'd tried to kill her not once, not twice, but three times, and he'd nearly succeeded.

With the lab coat fisted in one hand, he filled his other with his gun and slammed out of the trailer. Dusty and Devon stood side by side. Both men's eyes widened at the sight of him.

"Forest, my main man, don't do anything stupid here. Dillon is on his way," Dusty said hurriedly.

Forest didn't look at his friend. He kept his gaze focused like a laser beam on Devon. "Why?" The single word snapped out of him as he leveled his gun to Devon's midsection and threw the lab coat on the ground in front of him.

Devon feigned innocence with his eyes still widened behind his glasses. "What are you talking about? Why what?"

Forest barely clung to his control as he remembered Patience facedown on the ground after being hit in the back of the head and then faceup in the silo. As he thought of that night when he'd covered her with his own body to shield her from bullets that had come precariously close, his finger itched to shoot Devon, to make sure that the man could never harm Patience again.

"Why does your lab coat have a tear in it?" he asked.

Dusty sucked in a small breath while Devon feigned confusion. "A tear in my lab coat? I don't know, I might have caught it on a piece of equipment or ripped it on a jagged edge of a bone. These things happen…" His voice drifted off and he reached up to level his glasses on his nose.

"Or you tore it as you carried Patience's body up the silo ladder," Forest spat. A siren sounded in the distance, indicating Dillon was approaching quickly.

"I don't know what you're talking about," Devon replied with a touch of indignation. "Why on earth would I want to hurt Dr. Forbes?"

"I know it was you and I have the evidence in my pocket to prove it, and you're going to now tell me why." Forest cocked his gun.

At the same time, the siren stopped its scream as Dillon's vehicle squealed to a halt next to the trailer. He jumped out of the car and hurried toward where the three men stood.

"Forest, what's going on?" he asked with a forced calm.

"I'm considering putting a bullet through Devon's gut," Forest replied. "The only thing holding me back is that I want answers."

"Dillon, this man is obviously deranged," Devon said fervently. "You need to arrest him immediately."

"I think he's shown an incredible amount of control so far," Dusty said in Forest's defense.

"He's the person who has tried to kill Patience. He put her in the corn silo to die." Perspiration trickled down the center of Forest's back as he kept his gun pointed at Devon. "I've got the proof." He quickly explained to Dillon about the lab coat and the material he'd found.

"Forest, put your gun away. You don't want to make matters worse by forcing me to arrest you," Dillon said.

"I'm an unarmed man. If you shoot me it will be cold-blooded murder," Devon exclaimed.

Dusty placed a hand on Forest's shoulder. "Don't do it, man. Let Dillon take it from here."

Dillon pulled a set of handcuffs from his belt. "Besides," he said to Forest. "Your evidence will only add to the evidence I already have against Devon." He stepped closer to Devon. "Put your hands behind your back," he instructed.

"This is all nonsense," Devon said frantically as Dillon cuffed him.

"What evidence do you have?" Forest asked, his gun still in his hand and the itch to hurt Devon still like an irritating chigger burrowing deep inside him.

"Unfortunately for Devon, unlike the night he hit Patience over the head and she didn't see him, she remembered at the hospital that Devon had knocked on her door in the middle of the night. She distinctly remembers opening the door and seeing him before he slammed a needle in her and everything went black. He drugged her, and then when she was unconscious he carried her to the corn silo."

Devon's features transformed from confused innocence to twisted anger. "She deserved it. She deserved to die. Without her I wouldn't be an assistant, I'd be the top forensic anthropologist."

Forest finally lowered his gun and placed it back into its holster as Devon continued to spew hatred for the woman he worked for.

"She gets all the respect and I get none. She treats me like I'm nothing but a dumb hitchhiker she picked up along the road." Devon was practically frothing at the mouth. "I have the same credentials she has, I have the same education, yet because she's a young woman she got the top position. I hate her and I want her dead." He suddenly slammed his mouth closed, as if aware that he'd just dug his own grave.

"You won't be bothering Patience anymore," Dillon

said as he grabbed hold of Devon's elbow and began to lead him to the patrol car. "Maybe you can find a bone or two to examine in prison, because that's where you'll probably be spending the rest of your life."

He looked at Forest and Dusty. "Don't touch that lab coat and don't lose the material you found. I'll be back for them after I process Devon into jail."

Dillon placed the man in the back of the patrol car, and it was only as they drove off that Forest released a deep sigh of dispelled rage.

"He'll stand trial and the prosecutor has a good case to make sure he goes away for a very long time," Dusty said.

"Yeah, I know."

"Were you really going to shoot him?" Dusty asked.

Forest considered the question for a long moment. "To be honest, I don't know. I kept seeing flashes in my mind of Patience in that corn, of her lying on the ground unconscious, and there was a part of me that wanted to hurt Devon for hurting her." He smiled wryly at Dusty. "It's probably a good thing you called Dillon when you did."

"I didn't want to see you make a mistake that would affect the rest of your life," Dusty replied. "And now, there's work to be done. Are you going to the hospital to check in with Patience?"

"No." A pang shot off in Forest's heart. It was time for him to distance himself from the woman who had captured his love, a woman who had told him in no uncertain terms that she didn't want him in her life long-term.

"I think I'll head to my room for a shower. I'm covered in corn dust and sweat. After that I'll do a little work with Twilight." Surely working with the horse would calm the tumultuous emotions that filled him as he thought about everything that had happened and the fact that within the next day or two, he'd be forced to say goodbye to the woman he loved.

Patience left the hospital wearing a pair of Cassie's jeans and a blouse that the woman had brought to the hospital so that Patience wouldn't have to go home clad in the nasty purple nightgown she would never wear again.

It was dusk when the doctor had finally decided to release her, and she'd hesitated when it came to whom to call to take her home.

Her first impulse had been to call Forest, and she hadn't wanted to bother Dillon or any of his deputies. After giving it more thought, she'd decided to call Cassie. Other than Forest pulling her from the corn, the last conversation she'd had with him had not exactly been great.

Dillon had arrived back at the hospital several hours after bringing her in to let her know that Devon was behind bars and would be charged with attempted murder.

She still found it hard to believe that Devon had hated her so much he'd wanted her dead. He'd hidden his resentment of her well over their time working together.

"Are you sure you're feeling all right?" Cassie asked once they were in her car and headed to the ranch.

"Believe me, I've been pumped with enough fluids and food to last me a lifetime," Patience replied.

"So, I guess you'll finish up things tomorrow and leave the next day?"

"That's the plan," Patience replied. She stared out the passenger window where a lovers' sunset was splashed across the horizon. Oklahoma had a plethora of beautiful sunsets.

Now that the danger to her had passed, had Forest realized his love for her had only been the protectiveness of a nice man for a woman in danger?

She couldn't forget that moment when he'd pulled her from the corn and she'd gone down the ladder only to collapse on the ground and he hadn't come to her. She'd wanted him. She'd needed him, but he'd stepped away and kept his distance.

If she'd gone to tell him that she loved him the night before when she'd realized it, when she'd fully embraced it, she wouldn't have been in her room when Devon had appeared. The day would have gone quite differently.

Was it too late for her and Forest? She released a deep sigh. She didn't know. She only knew that when she'd needed his comfort he hadn't been there.

"I'm sure you're exhausted," Cassie said, mistaking the sigh for exhaustion rather than bittersweet regret.

"I was just thinking of what needed to be done so that I can finally get off your land," Patience replied.

Cassie flashed her a quick smile. "It's not that I want to see you go, but I'm definitely ready for that blue tent to disappear forever."

Patience returned her smile. "It will be up to Dillon

when that comes down, but other than writing final reports, my work here is finally done."

They pulled into the ranch entrance. "You don't have to drive me all the way to the rooms," Patience said. "I can walk from the driveway."

"Are you sure?" Cassie pulled down the lane and stopped the car in the driveway beside the main house.

"Positive. The walk will do me good, and at least now I don't have to worry about somebody jumping out of the shadows to attack me."

Cassie turned off the car engine. "It has to be a shock to know that it was Devon."

"It is a shock, but from what Dillon told me he was bitter that as a woman I had seniority." Patience shrugged. "I can't help what he believed, but I'm lead forensic anthropologist because my qualifications and field experience were better than his."

"At least you know you're safe now and things can get back to normal," Cassie said as the two got out of her car.

Normal? Patience didn't know what was normal anymore. Her entire world had been turned upside down by everything that had happened to her over the past twenty-four hours.

"Thanks for coming to get me. I really appreciate it," she said to Cassie. "I'll wash up your clothes and get them back to you tomorrow."

Cassie walked around the car, and to Patience's surprise, pulled her into her arms for an embrace. "I'm just so glad you're out of danger now." She released her hold and Patience stepped back, fighting against tears that threatened to fall.

"You have terrific men working here for you," she finally said as she swallowed against the tears.

"I know." Cassie looked in the direction of the cowboy "motel."

"It's impossible for me to believe that one of them is responsible for those old bones, for those poor victims."

"If there's an answer to be found, I'm sure Dillon will eventually get to the bottom of it." Patience thought of the ring she'd found at the base of the pit. Did it belong to a victim, or had the killer inadvertently left a clue? Dillon would have his hands full trying to get real answers.

"Good night, Cassie, and thanks again for everything." Cassie murmured a goodnight and Patience began the long walk to her room.

Immediately her mind filled with thoughts of Forest. He hadn't soothed her when she'd collapsed and he hadn't called to check on her during the hours she'd been at the hospital.

But then why would he? She'd made it quite clear to him the night before that she wanted nothing to do with him or his love. She'd refused his heart when he'd tried to give it to her.

Light spilled out of his room, and her heart ached with the need to tell him that he'd made her believe in love, that he'd taught her so many life lessons and she wanted to live the rest of her life with him.

She had no idea how he might feel about her now, and she feared speaking her heart to him and being rejected.

But she feared more never speaking her heart to him and leaving here not knowing what might have been.

Without giving herself time to overthink it or chicken out, she knocked on his door. He answered, his eyes blue depths of deep, still waters. "Patience, I'm glad you're okay."

"The doctors released me a little while ago and Cassie came to get me. It's still early. I was wondering if you'd want to sit out here with me for a little while?" She held her breath. His features held no emotion.

He hesitated and then finally nodded. "Okay." He stepped back inside the room and grabbed the two chairs they always used.

She sank into one and he placed his just close enough that she could smell the clean scent with a hint of familiar cologne that clung to him.

They sat in silence for so long her chest tightened and her mouth dried. Funny, she'd never had a problem blurting out frustrations or anger, but she was ridiculously nervous about speaking of her love.

"Rough day for you," he finally said to break the silence.

"Yes, but thank God you found me when you did." She thought about how long she'd been certain she was going to die. "I had resigned myself to death, but I also had lots of time to think while I was waiting to die."

"Sometimes that can be a good thing and sometimes it can be a bad thing," he replied. "I mean the 'having too much time to think' thing." He kept his focus in the distance, not looking at her.

"Forest?" She waited until his gaze slowly moved to

look at her. "I want to tell you about last night. I want to talk about how we left things between us."

His eyes narrowed just a bit. "I figure there isn't much left to talk about. We both had our say and that's that." His sexy lips compressed into a taut line.

"I thought I had my say, but I realize now I'm not finished and I don't like that, I don't like it one bit," she replied. He was so handsome on the outside, with his dark hair, blue eyes and sculptured features. She was physically drawn to him with a passion, but it was the man beneath the skin who had forever changed her.

"Then I suppose you'd better have your say and be done with it," he replied. He crossed his arms over his chest, as if forming a formidable defense against her.

"I went back to my room last night and I did a lot of thinking. I thought about my parents and how my life has played out, how I'd been taught to deal only in facts and how I'd used anger to keep people away. You changed all that, Forest."

His gaze held hers intently, although she still couldn't get a feel about what he might be thinking, how he might be feeling about her.

"You taught me to allow people into my life, to open myself up to lovers' sunsets and the intangibles that have no basis in fact, they just are. You made me understand that anger isn't the way to communicate emotions."

"I'm glad." His features softened slightly. "Your life will be better, richer if you open yourself up." He offered her a small smile. "People in Oklahoma City won't recognize you when you go home."

"That's just the thing… I don't want to go home, at least not alone. It will never be home again, not unless you're there with me." She drew in a deep breath for courage. "I love you, Forest. That's what I finally recognized last night. I opened my heart and looked inside and all I could see was my love for you."

He remained so still she wondered if he'd really heard her, or if it was too late and he didn't want to hear any words of love from her.

"This morning when I was so certain death was imminent, all I wanted was a vision of you in my head as I died. I am in love with you and I want your children and I want a happily-ever-after with you," she continued fervently.

He unfolded his arms and leaned forward, his eyes glowing in the moonlight. "You have to be sure, Patience. You have to be very sure. I only want to do this once and it has to be right."

"I've never been more certain of anything in my entire life," she replied and held his gaze intently.

He studied her for a long moment and then stood. Patience's heart sank. Was he going back inside his room? Was this truly the end?

"What I don't understand is if you love me and I love you, then why in the hell aren't we kissing right now," he said.

Patience's heart exploded with happiness as she jumped out of her chair and into his arms. His mouth took hers with a sweet possession she welcomed, one that she wanted for the rest of her life.

When the kiss finally ended, she gazed up at him with a smile. "I like this. I like this so much."

"Finally, something you like," he said with a wonderfully carefree laugh.

"Finally, somebody I love," she added.

His lips took hers once again, this time with a fiery passion that she trusted would last a lifetime. She didn't need facts or scientific evidence to know that Forest was her happily-ever-after.

He sang through her heart, the organ she'd always believed was just for pumping blood. He rang in her soul, a place she hadn't believed existed until now, and her mind teemed with endless possibilities of a future filled with love…and Forest.

Epilogue

Patience pulled the huge white lab vehicle out of the Holiday Ranch entrance. She'd written her final reports and turned everything over to Dillon. She'd said all of her goodbyes to the men and to Cassie and had to admit that there was a touch of bittersweet sadness at leaving what had become such a magical place to her.

However her true magic traveled in a navy blue pickup just behind her. In the two days since they had declared their love for one another, Forest had not only packed up all of his belongings, but he'd also contacted a Realtor in Oklahoma City to check out ranches for sale just outside the city limits.

Patience would continue her work with the Oklahoma Police Department and lecture occasionally at the college. The only difference was that eventually when everything was settled, she would be traveling to work from a ranch house instead of her apartment. Once they found the ranch where they would be building their future, Forest would return to the Holiday place to trailer Thunder and bring her to live on his ranch.

In the meantime Forest would be staying with her in her apartment. She didn't care if they had to live in a tent as long as they were in it together.

She glanced in her rearview mirror, her heart blossoming at the sight of him in the vehicle behind her. In the past two days they had talked of their love and made love, as well as planned a future that welled up inside her a happiness she'd never known before.

She was going to give her big, lonely cowboy everything he'd mourned when he'd lost his family. She would be the partner in life that he'd wanted, she would give him children that would fill their lives with joy and laughter and whenever possible she'd give him pot roast Sundays.

Her heart was fully open, not only to accepting friendship and love, but to giving it as well. She stepped on the gas, eager to get to Oklahoma City and her future with her friend, her lover…her Forest.

Dillon sat at his desk in his office in the quiet small Bitterroot police station. His door was closed, and before him on his desk blotter was the ring that Patience had found in the pit.

The day that Patience had disappeared, he'd had to cancel his appointment with Francine Rogers, and in the past two days he'd been busy dealing with paperwork, evidence and transfer orders to remove Devon from the Bitterroot jail to one in Oklahoma City. Devon had been picked up that morning in a transport vehicle with three police guards.

With that issue resolved, Dillon was back to the bigger issue of the mass grave and seven victims. He was meeting with Francine later this afternoon, eager to get any and all information the social worker might possess as to the young men she'd brought to Cass's ranch to work.

His gut instinct was that the killer was still here, in Bitterroot, possibly on the Holiday or the Humes ranch. Despite his soft feelings toward Cassie, and the respect he'd had for Cass, even the dead woman was a potential suspect in the murders that had taken place so long ago.

He picked up the ring that was encased in a small plastic evidence bag. He was determined to somehow, someway find the owner and ultimately find the killer, no matter who got hurt in the process.

* * * * *

MILLS & BOON®

INTRIGUE
Romantic Suspense

A SEDUCTIVE COMBINATION OF DANGER AND DESIRE

A sneak peek at next month's titles...

In stores from 14th January 2016:

Scene of the Crime: Who Killed Shelly Sinclair? – Carla Cassidy *and* **Blue Ridge Ricochet** – Paula Graves
Bulletproof Badge – Angi Morgan *and*
Fully Committed – Janie Crouch
Colorado Wildfire – Cassie Miles *and*
Suspect Witness – Ryshia Kennie

Romantic Suspense

A Secret in Conard County – Rachel Lee
Colton's Surprise Heir – Addison Fox

MILLS & BOON®

**If you enjoyed this story,
you'll love the the full *Revenge Collection*!**

MILLS & BOON®
The Billionaires Collection!

This fabulous 6 book collection features stories from some of our talented writers. Feel the temperature rise with our ultra-sexy and powerful billionaires. Don't miss this great offer – buy the collection today to get two books free!

Order yours at
**www.millsandboon.co.uk
/billionaires**

MILLS & BOON®

Man of the Year

Our winning cover star will be revealed next month!

**Don't miss out on your copy
– order from millsandboon.co.uk**

Read more about Man of the Year 2016 at

www.millsandboon.co.uk/moty2016

**Have you been following our
Man of the Year 2016 campaign?**
🐦 **#MOTY2016**

MILLS & BOON®

Want to get more from Mills & Boon?

Here's what's available to you if you join the
exclusive **Mills & Boon eBook Club** today:

Convenience – choose your books each month
Exclusive – receive your books a month before
anywhere else
Flexibility – change your subscription at any time
Variety – gain access to eBook-only series
Value – subscriptions from just £3.99 a month

o visit **www.millsandboon.co.uk/esubs** today
to be a part of this exclusive eBook Club!